Please Don't Go Offshore Daddy

DAVID P. MATHESON

Please Don't

Go

Offshore Daddy

DAVID P. MATHESON

Introduction

With thanks to all my offshore friends and colleagues who shared their experiences with me during the writing of this novel.

The offshore environment is a unique but often complicated and dangerous place to work.

Working offshore means also *living* offshore, with people you like and people you do not! We rely on each other for companionship, and ultimately survival.

The characters in this book are fictional; any resemblance to actual people is purely coincidental. But hey, if you are friends with anyone who happens to resemble one of the characters, then lucky you for having such interesting friends!

David.

The Author

David P. Matheson works offshore. He has many years of experience working with people in remote locations.

He writes for a hobby, mostly during the evenings in his cabin after work.

David was born in Toryglen, Glasgow in 1966. He attended John Bosco Secondary School in the Gorbals, after which he pursued a medical career which has taken him too many corners of the planet, some good and some not so good.

Just a thought..................

Before you decide to read the book can I ask you to *look again* at the men and woman who work offshore.

We are not all beer swigging wasters who pish our money up against the wall.

We do not all have problems with alcohol.

Some of us are intelligent creative and passionate individuals, some of us are also as *thick as mince*.

It is a job and a life style, but beneath the oily overalls and hard hats are stories to be told, of *'who we really are.'*

Chapters

1. Those early morning check-ins.
2. The importance of a postcode.
3. Galley wars.
4. A tangled web we weave.
5. So your wife is a 'male' then.
6. The unexpected 'porn king'.
7. Their life is never as perfect as they say.
8. Whatever it takes.
9. A sweaty gym bench.
10. Do we ever *really* know our partners?
11. A gay wedding is on.
12. Two sides to every story.

13. Things are never as they seem.

14. The tool pusher is 'coming out'.

15. The septic tank is full of surprises.

16. What's in a name?

17. A visit from the police.

18. Some people are just pathetic.

19. Where are they now?

Terms and abbreviations

Boot room: Changing room, coffee room.

Galley: Kitchen/dining hall.

Heli Admin: Helicopter lounge where crew depart or arrive.

OIM: Offshore Installation Manager (Rig Boss).

Third party: Visiting crew, non-permanent to the rig.

Tool pusher: Shift supervisor.

Steward/Stewardess: Catering staff.

Vantage: An offshore computer system that records the movements of personnel, personal details, next of kin etc. It is security protected and only selected personnel have access to it.

That Early Morning Check Ins....

Alec crawled out of bed and threw the little red alarm clock across the room, leaving another black mark on the white walls. He could have used the marks to calculate each time he had left his bed to go offshore; he always had the same feeling.

"Oh for fuck's sake," he scolded himself as he turned on the cold tap instead of the hot. The room was cold. It was 4.30am. "I hate early check-ins," he muttered under his breath as he put his face up to the showerhead to try and stimulate his eyes to open and focus.

Alec looked in the mirror; he needed a shave, the first in three weeks. He was a good-looking man and appeared younger than his 45 years, with some laughter lines but very few grey hairs in his cropped black hair. He held his stomach in and peered at his reflection. He was still toned and almost athletic, but his little protruding belly gave away his lack of exercise. *Must pack my trainers and use the gym more often this trip,* he thought. He looked again in the mirror.

"Who am I kidding?" he said, half expecting the reflection to answer back.

He sneaked up the stairs and into his son's room. Joshua was in a deep sleep, his blonde hair just visible at the top of his *Thomas the Tank Engine* duvet with his hair spouting out of Henry's funnel. It made Alec smile. He kissed Joshua on the forehead and left. He passed his bedroom and hesitated. His wife Katrina was still asleep; she had been a complete bitch to him during this leave. *Fuck her,* he thought. Alec saw the taxi coming down the drive. He checked for his passport, his Vantage card and left.

The helicopter reception area was busy. Across the room, in a strong cockney accent, came a welcoming voice.

"Alec, ya sweet wee Jock, over here lad." He turned with a smile and waved at his pal Terry who was on the other side of the room.

"Over in a minute, just getting sorted out first." Alec checked in and followed the routine. He looked at the screen at his next of kin. There she was his wife of seventeen years and still his next of kin. He had no idea why; he often looked at her wondering who the hell she was, and he did the same here at check-in.

"Check your details on the screen sir," said the bleary-eyed check-in girl. *Probably scrubs up really well,* he thought, *but looks like a bag of shit like the rest of us this time in the morning.* He made polite conversation with security then went to join Terry. He accepted the gentle slap across the face and the twist of the nipples from Terry which was his way of saying 'hello'.

Terry and Alec had worked together for seven years on the same rig. There was very little either man didn't know about the other. Some things they discussed with others on the rig, others they kept to themselves.

Terry and Alec were both 45. At 6ft 3in, Terry towered above Alec's 5ft 8in frame. He was toned and fit, with daily visits to the gym being just as important as the oxygen he breathed to stay alive. His head was shaved which emphasised his square jaw. His piercing blue eyes complemented his bronze tan acquired in Tenerife where he now lived with his partner.

"Good flight over then?" asked Alec as he took a cup of coffee from the vending machine. "How's Stephen getting on with the new job?"

Stephen was Terry's partner, a confidence Terry had shared only with Alec. He thought it an unsafe bet to share his homosexuality with others on the rig. Terry hated that, but that was just the way it was.

Alec had been surprised when Terry had told him of his sexuality as there was not a camp bone in Terry's body. Alec thought people's sexual orientation unimportant; life was about people and he was certainly not a man to judge.

The men often joked about how people 'changed' going offshore or how they became somebody else once the flight suit went on.

Respectable men and women turned into gargoyles, swearing, shouting and using the most inappropriate language with each other which they would never use at home and yet the response would be laughter. If someone called you a 'sweaty fat twat' across a room in an office or in other places of work, it may well result in disciplinary action. This was acceptable offshore; in fact, verbal abuse could often be seen as a compliment.

"The job's going really well, he seems to enjoy it. Not my thing but as long as he keeps the costume at work and the Euros coming in, long may it last," laughed Terry.

Terry and Stephen had moved to Tenerife to get away from the torrent of abuse they had received in their small home counties village. They had been hounded out by the local anti-gay louts which Terry suspected was fuelled by their two nice cars and smart postcode. They had sold up and moved to 'The Reef'.

Stephen had taken a job as a singer but it was several months before he had confessed to Terry that he was performing as a transvestite, a secret he had managed to keep for four months due to Terry's offshore schedule. He had found out during a weekend visit from Stephen's mother. Terry was more pissed off that Stephen's very nice but interfering mother had told him.

They had spent the next few days making ground rules. Terry thought the transvestite scene horrendous, but accepted this was Stephen's job and his way of contributing to the household income.

He had ranted when he found out – "Can you not get a fucking job in a bar or a hotel instead of dressing like a big poof and wearing high heels?" He had stormed around the villa shouting at Stephen after his mother had made a swift exit to the shops.

"Fuck off you! I'm a big poof, so are you," retorted Stephen.

That comment had reduced both men to laughter and the argument was done.

Stephen was much more open about being gay, having known since he was a teenager. Terry was more reserved; he had known since his early teens but having worked offshore since he was 18, he had closeted this part of his life. He was so far into his closet he was almost at the 'White Witch's Castle' in Narnia!

Offshore, he still referred to Stephen as his partner, and if ever questioned for a name, he would be 'Stephanie'.

The Importance of A Post Code

"Here comes the birdie," said Maryanne, the rig medic.

She was standing at the window in heli admin watching the clouds and praying the wind wouldn't pick up and cause the flight to be cancelled. Maryanne had worked on the rig for seven years; having reached 40 and still single, she had left the NHS, disillusioned with the pay and conditions.

She was tall and slim, her brown hair tied up on top of her head. She wore only a little make-up, just enough to make her seem less tired and worn-looking. Her huge brown eyes were captivating which she used to her benefit when offshore. She liked the rig, she was happy there.

She had secured her place in the team, working hard to establish some respect in the male-oriented world. She had conquered many men during her seven years on the rig, but waited until the end of the trip before bedding them in a hotel. She didn't want to be known as the 'rig bike' and she certainly didn't want a relationship. She had a good life, a nice home and a healthy bank account. She never dated where she lived but preferred her one-night stands at the airport hotel before heading home to Surrey. She did plan ahead and on most occasions she got whatever 'willie' she wanted, but some needed more teasing than others.

She watched as the passengers walked from the helicopter making their way down to the arrivals lounge.

Her pupils dilated and her loins tingled when she saw Terry. She liked him but he had ignored her when she had raised her game and suggested a drink in the hotel before he flew home to Tenerife. She considered Terry to be noble but she liked a challenge. If she had to bed Alec to get to Terry, she would. She knew Alec had a crap relationship and it wouldn't take much to get him to bed.

Like a lot of offshore men, their wives just used them as a cash machine. Not all of them, but many did.

It amused Maryanne when men tried to get her to pity them with their stories of wives who were bitches or girlfriends who had been cheating on them whilst they worked hard offshore.

These blokes worked hard trying to get her sympathy in the hope they would get a' shag'. They had no idea that she already had her knickers in her pocket; she was 'working' them. She felt like a manipulative cow sometimes, but she was always tickled by how easy it was to bed even 'Mr Faithful'. Her mother would have called her a whore but she just thought herself as highly-sexed.

Terry knew what Maryanne was all about; he was gay but he could see her game. He was certainly not stupid. He did like her and considered her to be one of his friends on the rig. He gave her a kiss as he entered heli admin, making chit-chat as he took his transit suit off.

"Will she ever fuck off?" he whispered to Alec.

"Doubt it lad, you know how she is, a stalker until she gets your spunk."

Maryanne shot at a glance at the men as they chuckled over their remarks.

Alec thought of phoning Katrina as he passed the line of people waiting to use the phone. He was lucky he had his own line in his office.

Fuck her he thought. She can phone me, and she will when she is skint.

Katrina stretched and yawned. She never noticed that Alec had gone, she couldn't care less. She put the kettle on and made a coffee. She had fifteen minutes before Joshua needed to be up for school. She took her phone from the bedside table where it had been charging and curled up on the sofa. There was a message from Sam. She smiled as she sipped her coffee.

She wrote a text. "Meet me tomorrow at 8pm outside McAdoo's pub on the high street. 'Twat face' gets paid tomorrow so we can have a meal and do a club. Josh is going to my mother's for the weekend." She pressed 'send'.

The reply was swift. "No bother. 8pm."

The sitting room was modern. Katrina had chosen the entire decor for this house as Alec never seemed interested in interior design. He spent his time at home with Joshua, or working in the garage building his model aeroplanes and selling them on *eBay*. It irritated the hell out of her. The plasma TV on the wall above the fire was on mute as Lorraine Kelly chatted to some wannabe from a reality show.

There were no curtains at the windows, just white venetian blinds. A nest of pine tables sat in the corner. The house was a nice detached new build. She liked that. Her *goal* on marrying Alec was to go from a flat to a two bedroom house, finally reaching a four bedroom detached. Katrina was where she wanted to be in life. She couldn't care less that it was at Alec's expense. She didn't like objet d'art or pictures; the room was minimally furnished and even the toys had to be put away in the hall cupboard. Her mother thought the room looked like a mortuary.

Katrina and Alec had been married for seventeen years. It had been fun for a while. She thought she could cope with offshore life, plenty of the neighbours did. She so wanted the detached house and the two cars in the driveway. She had herself the perfect postcode. Nothing and nobody mattered; the postcode was all she needed.

Katrina finished her coffee and got Joshua ready for school. He looked so like his dad it scared her sometimes; she felt like she was talking to Alec when she looked into Joshua's eyes, stunningly blue and clear just like his father's. She couldn't deny that her husband was a good catch – handsome, funny and a big fat salary. She had a little part-time job in a garage two hours a week. It paid for her weekly hairdressing trip, her nails and her manicures.

She waved to the neighbours as she left the drive with the car roof down. Joshua liked that and so did she. Her peroxide blonde hair was blowing in the wind, she felt good, she looked forty-something – a little bit well-used thought Alec – but she liked the blonde look.

"I hate this uniform," wailed Joshua, "it's itchy and horrible. Why do I need to wear a tie? Liam next door wears a T-shirt and fleece to school. Why can't I?"

He took his straw boater hat off his head. "The elastic hurts my chin. I hate this hat," he protested.

Katrina was putting her lipstick on as they waited to join the dual carriageway.

"We've been over this a million times, you know the rules, and Dad has explained we want you to have a good start in life, we have explained to you that the school is the best in the area."

She tried to put his hat back on his head whilst he protested, with one hand on the steering wheel.

"The *peasant children* from next door will get rubbish jobs; you will make the most money and have lots of fast cars while they wait for the bus."

Joshua had his fingers in his ears and his eyes tight shut.

"Dad works very hard to pay for you to go to this school, so don't be ungrateful and put your hat on this instant! We are about to pass the bus stop and I can see Jessica Linthorpe with her daughter waiting for the bus. That poor girl, having to go to the local comprehensive."

They waited in the stagnant queue of traffic, it was always the same. The oil industry was buoyant, and so was the construction of new housing estates outside Aberdeen. The once green fields where now a sea of urban housing developments.

As they waited to join the main traffic she took Joshua's hat and put it on his head. She slowed down and waved at Jessica Linthorpe. Jessica waved back reluctantly. Her husband had worked offshore with Alec several years ago; he had left her for a younger woman, refusing to pay the mortgage or any bills. The house had been repossessed and she was now back living with her parents.

Katrina was pleased that Alec had agreed that their son should go to a private school in Aberdeen. It was a 25-minute drive each way. She cared nothing of the little boy's protests, or that Joshua had no friends on their estate as all the other kids went to the local primary school.

She insisted that he kept his blazer and hat on when they went shopping; for her, his uniform was an important accessory. No matter how hot the weather, his uniform was as important as designer handbags or shoes.

Galley Wars

Todd was tired. He had been offshore for two weeks, only a week to go. He hated getting up and always left it to the very last minute. He would miss a shower and run to the boot room for shift handover with seconds to spare. He rushed through the door and into the room not knowing that Patrick Kelly, the OIM, was behind the door. The sudden push of the door sent Patrick across the room, knocking him into a very tired and 'always angry' roustabout, known as 'Ugly'.

"Oh for Christ's sake, you stupid, smelly, dirty little worm. What's your excuse this time?" shouted Patrick as Todd fiddled with his overalls in embarrassment.

"Sorry boss, I overslept."

The room erupted in laughter and Todd blushed. He squeezed his way into a corner and waited for handover to begin. Ugly spat on the floor and glared at Todd.

Shit, I'm in for a hard shift, thought Todd.

When Patrick Kelly had gone, Ugly passed Todd, saying nothing but going close enough to kiss him. His unshaven stubble almost touching Todd's skin. He growled instead. Todd tried a wry smile.

This was Todd's first trip offshore.

He had dropped out of university having failed his accountancy course. His father worked at head office and had secured his son a job. Todd was tall and lanky, no common sense, but very intelligent.

Ugly stopped and turned to Todd.

"Put your boots on the correct feet before you go outside boy," he snarled. Todd looked down at his feet, blushing at his stupidity. The night was just getting worse.

Maryanne breezed into the room on her way to the galley.

"Evening spunk bucket!" shouted Ugly as he turned to leave the room.

"Piss off you horrible little man," retaliated Maryanne in her Surrey accent. *There's even a bit of cockney in there when she's angry,* thought Ugly.

"Aww, come on girly, I'm old but still worth one," laughed Ugly.

Maryanne pushed her nose in the air and breezed out of the room, leaving a pungent smell of perfume as she went.

The galley was busy.

Meal times came around too fast for Nancy. She was the cook, and answered to the 'camp boss' otherwise known as the catering manager. *It's not a bloody picnic,* she would think. *Camp boss? More like being in the brownies, not on an oil rig.*

The camp boss was called Malcolm, also known as 'minger Malcolm' amongst the crew as they thought he constantly smelt of 'pish'.

He had been offshore for 20 years and every trip he reminded Nancy that her five years were nothing compared to his experience. He was annoying her tonight with his bloody budget.

"Nine pounds a head you stupid cow. I said nine pounds, not nine thousand," repeated Malcolm. She had used some almost out-of-date remnants of baking materials to make some cakes as a treat; he thought she had used next week's stores. He threw the baking tray across the kitchen, nearly hitting Andrea the stewardess who then ran out crying.

"Piss off you stupid bag," he bellowed as the girl ran from the Galley.

Nancy never ever ran from anyone. She had grown up in Glasgow and could handle herself.

"Right, you stupid, fat, grey-haired old sod. I told you I know its nine pounds a head, you tell me every frigin' day!" she screamed at Malcolm. Her voice bounced off the walls and back into her ears, making her dizzy.

She took the knife from the wall and scowled at Malcolm.

"I've just about had enough of you, it's time you went to meet your maker," she snarled with her teeth clenched tight shut. She was only 5ft tall, slim and, on first take, vulnerable. Her green eyes complemented her red frizzy hair which she attempted to secure under her cap, but the fight was useless as the ginger locks could be seen tumbling out of each side. She was a pretty woman.

Malcolm moved slowly around the island in the middle of the kitchen.

He was a short man with a huge heavy belly, his little blue cap sitting on his bald head with strands of grey sticking out from above his ears. He had a bulbous nose, a rugged complexion and few teeth. The pair of them fought all the time but Nancy had never gone for the knife.

Malcolm jumped into the refrigerator and slammed the door; he held the handle tight so she couldn't open it. Nancy took a table and pushed it against the handle. She placed the knife back in its holder, picked up her cigarettes and left.

Ten minutes passed. Malcolm was cold, very cold. He tried the door.

Nothing happened, it wouldn't move. He began to panic, banging on the door and shouting for help. The OIM heard the noise from the galley as he poured a cup of coffee. The kitchen was empty. *Break-time,* he thought. He heard the raised voice and the banging.

He pushed the table away from the door. As Patrick opened the door, Malcolm was about to bang again, instead he tumbled out the door into a heap on the floor at Patrick's feet. The OIM took his coffee and stepped over Malcolm. He said nothing and left.

Nancy was in the laundry talking to the stewardess who had just come on night shift. She spotted Malcolm's laundry.

"Oh don't bother taking Malcolm's laundry up to his cabin, I'll drop it off on my way up to the smoke room." Smiled Nancy.

Nancy climbed the stairs to the 5th level where her cabin was. She opened the door at the end of the corridor that led onto the stair well outside, her only taste of fresh air she got in her day.

She stood for a while watching the sun bow behind the horizon. It was a beautiful evening.

She scanned the deck area. Not a person in sight.

She lifted Malcolm's bag of laundry that was tied securely with a fastener. She threw the full bag into the sea and went back inside.

Malcolm never asked for his laundry, he knew he had pushed his luck.

A typical galley day.

A Hump In A Tub

Katrina was waiting by the window, the taxi was booked for half eight. She looked the best she could. Her red dress was tight, stopping mid-thigh, the collar cut down to her cleavage and the same at the back. Her black high heels matched her bag. Her hair was up and she felt good. Her mum came through from the kitchen. She took Joshua to the car and placed his little bag in the boot.

She went back to the front door where Katrina was waiting for the taxi.

"For Christ's sake Katrina, you're 44. You look like a prostitute, not a wife and mother." She got in the car and left the drive way.

Katrina waited until the car was gone, then she gave her mother the 'one middle finger' sign, being sure her mother could not see her do it. She couldn't fall out with her; she was a great babysitter, even at short notice.

Sam was already waiting for her at the pub door. She kissed him passionately then wiped the lipstick from his face. He might be ten years younger than her and have no job but he was great in bed and that's what she wanted. She was in control of him.

Sam was in his 30s. He had never held down a job for more than a month. Instead, he had turned into the equivalent of a male prostitute, working his way into the lives of women who had nothing better to do than spend their money on him. He made enough to make a living. He just drifted along enjoying the ride. He knew he was good-looking, naturally charming and a brilliant liar. He never took a woman back to his flat; that was his refuge.

Katrina had already booked a room at the Cultcliff Ranks Hotel – the usual room with spa and champagne. They had a quick drink in the pub then headed for the hotel.

She knew she looked like a slut, but that's what Sam wanted; she was the prostitute, not him, and the looks from the reception staff confirmed this guise had worked. She paid the bill but they gave the keys to Sam, avoiding eye contact with Katrina.

In the far corner of the lobby the night cleaner was dusting the grand piano. She watched as Katrina strutted to the lift in her high heels with her arm linked in Sam's. Jessica Linthorpe polished slowly as she watched Sam put his hand up Katrina's skirt; she could see she had no knickers on, or if she was wearing a thong it must have been so far up her backside she could use it to floss her teeth.

Jessica slipped back behind the piano out of sight.

The room was big. The bed was round and sat in the middle of the floor. The spa was already running when they arrived, just as Katrina had requested.

She took off her dress and climbed into the tub. Sam watched her reflection in the window as he looked out across the city. She was older than he preferred, a bit saggy around the edges, and she talked too much for his liking. She paid him £200 for a few hours' sex, and the bonus was that she liked it rough. Katrina only ever had sex with Sam immediately after Alec had left; she needed time for the bruises to go.

Sam walked to the edge of the bath.

"Hey slut, look at you in the bubbles." Katrina gave him a smile that was her non-verbal 'do it'.

He grabbed her by the hair and pulled her out the bath, his other hand covering her mouth to dull her screams. He dragged her across the floor and threw her in a heap. She was face down on the carpet.

Sam took off his shoes and put his foot behind her neck. He took his belt from his trousers and whipped her bare bottom. She was shaking with pain. He knelt beside her putting his knee into the back of her neck. He removed his clothes and grabbed her by the shoulders quickly turning her over on to her back. Then, Sam stuffed his sock in Katrina's mouth. He waited a few seconds to make sure she was breathing through her nostrils. He tied her hands together and secured them with his belt to the leg of the bed. He then had sex with her. He didn't enjoy it, but he gave her what she wanted – rough, dirty sex.

They never really had a conversation; he just screwed her, roughed her up a bit, got paid and went. They communicated more by text.

Katrina tried to make herself look presentable before leaving, but by now she looked like she had been dragged through a bush twice over. She got in a taxi and went home.

Sam made a call. Off he went to meet Sarah, another lonely offshore wife, and another easy £200.

A Tangled Web We Weave...

Steven enjoyed his job as the safety rep on board the rig.

He was well-liked, polite and helpful. The son of a black Jamaican dad and a white Jamaican mother, he would considered himself a 'Caucasian male' with dark colouring. He had a scar running from his left ear to the corner of his left mouth, his 'war wound' from climbing trees as a child was his answer if asked how it happened. He kept his tight 'salt and pepper 'curly hair short.

He had been on the rig three years. No one knew his story, or at least the real one. He had come to work on the rig after a job in the Australian mines. At least in his head he had.

In reality, Steven had been released from prison six months before coming offshore, using his 'resettlement' to pay for his entire offshore course fee. He tried to forget about his past.

At just 22, he had gone to prison for manslaughter. He served 21 years. It had been national news – he was the burglar who had given an old man such a fright that he'd had a heart attack and died. Steven had not been violent but he was soon tracked down by the police. His sentence was not 'life' as the death was not intentional. His family had disowned him so he had begun a new life offshore. He lived in London. He hated it but it was the best place to be anonymous, so that's where he had settled. He went into heli admin to meet with Maryanne.

"Morning Steven," she chirped across the desk, flashing a smile in his direction. "Flight's in twenty minutes, seven new crew coming on."

Steven always worried that someone might recognise him from his past. Maryanne hoped her end-of-trip shag would be on the flight.

Neither shared their thoughts.

Brendan Hastings was the driller on duty. They had stopped drilling as the helicopter came into land on the rig.

"Gotta disappear for five minutes," he shouted to Mateo the assistant driller. "Cover the job will you? If you fuck it up, I'll kill you." He was serious.

Mateo took the seat in the driller's console; he could feel excitement in his loins as he sat on the driller's throne.

Brendan went to the phone booth and shut the door. He took out his diary and dialled the number. His wife Carona answered.

"Happy birthday!" he shouted in an excited voice down the phone. "Oh Brendan," Carona replied in sultry Spanish tones, "it's not today, its next month, the eighteenth *next* month." They chatted a while then said their goodbyes. Brendan wiped the sweat from his forehead. It was mid-November and cold but he was sweating like a chicken in an oven. He dialled another number. Emma answered the phone.

"Hey Brendan, how's you?" came the quiet English woman's voice. He could hear the baby crying in the background; it was his son.

"Happy birthday honey!" said Brendan.

"Aww thanks pet, you're the best husband anyone could wish for," said Emma his wife.

He never meant to have two wives, it just sort of happened. Deep down he loved the thrill and excitement of it all, but at the back of his mind he knew he was a *bigamist*, in fact if he was honest he knew he was a *bloody bastard*.

When the call was over, Brendan took a seat in heli admin. He chatted briefly with Steven and Maryanne.

He thought again about how close he had come to slipping up. Having two wives was hard work; a wife and two kids in Spain and a wife with a newborn in Cornwall. Keeping out of prison for bigamy was harder. He passed a wink to Maryanne as he left.

The seven passengers settled into the induction. Maryanne stalked around the room for her next duvet partner, whilst Steven was relieved no one recognised him.

The day went on.

The Unlikely
'Parn King'

Jessica Linthorpe was at the bus stop again in her supermarket uniform, seeing her daughter off to school. Supermarket by day, hotel cleaner by night. That was her life with some cat napping in between.

She had no memory of the last time she had slept a whole night in her bed, her daughter was now virtually raised by her parents. She was never home. She needed to earn, to save, and to get a place of her own.

She was 38 years old and certainly attractive; her brown hair was curly and sat nicely on her shoulders. Jessica hardly ever did the hairdresser thing; she never really needed to. Her fresh complexion made her look younger than she was. She had lost a lot of weight since her separation but, as her parents would often assure her, that was a good thing. Her father told her to forget "that bastard of a husband" and move on. She was trying to. She was back in the house where she grew up, in the bed she had slept in since she was 12 years old. She was grateful to her parents, but needed to move on.

Jessica saw *the tart* in her car with the miserable-looking little boy in his silly over-the-top uniform and ridiculous hat. He was his father's double. She took her opportunity as the car stopped in traffic at the bus stop.

"Hi Katrina, we must do coffee soon, loads to catch up on." *Yes, you dirty bitch, we have loads to catch up on,* she thought.

"Great idea, I'll meet you tomorrow at noon in the supermarket café, save you the bus fare going into town," replied Katrina, flicking her hair and flashing a bitchy smile. She did not enjoy the company of younger and prettier woman. She had chosen her friends carefully. They were much fatter than she, certainly uglier, and they *had to* be poorer than her. She needed to be the centre of attention on a 'girl's night out.

She briefly remembered Alec asking why she had chosen her ugliest and fattest friends, some she barely knew to be her bridesmaids at their wedding, over the years he had worked it out.

"See you then," answered Jessica smiling. *If only you knew what I know, you cheap whore.*

Morgan Pearson had worked as a mechanic on this rig for seven years and had been with the company for many more. He was a quiet and unassuming man. He blended into the crowd. He liked it that way.

Morgan had moved to one of the Scottish islands from his home in Birmingham, but he still visited the city regularly to see family.

That was his story.

He was in his 50s and married with two grown-up boys. He had a picture of them on his locker in his cabin. They were a happy family. He and his wife had good holidays; his kids both had their own flats in Aberdeen which he had funded. Their life was good.

His second income certainly helped.

Morgan was in his cabin. He flipped open his laptop and logged in to his emails. His 'Inbox' was full with lots of attachments which was a normal occurrence. Hundreds of emails from people he had never met. He scrolled through them, clicking randomly on the images, some he deleted, others he saved.

There were some familiar faces in a few of the pictures, people still trying to make it. He felt sorry for them. He had been doing this for years, so he could tell who was suitable and who was not.

"Crikey, some of these pictures; how the hell do they manage these positions?" he said in surprise. Even after all these years, some still shocked him. He sat on the little seat next to his single bed. The cabin was small but he had a single room and he was grateful for that. He had seen plenty of people offshore who would be perfect for his other line of work, but he never mixed the two together. That would be suicidal.

Morgan clicked on the desktop icon, 'Rancoon Productions'.

He scrolled through the site; he had made £2000 in ten days – that was good, not the best, but good.

He sold porn. In fact, he made porn. He worked as a producer under the name 'Rancoon Ravatt.'

The name would come up at the start of many hundreds of porn movies, along with other made-up names such as 'Mandy Munches' and 'Dillon Dildo' and many more. He was always amused at the screen names that people would think up. He worked out of a house he owned in Birmingham; he did camera work and production but never took part in any of the activities. He found it all very distasteful, but a great little earner. His wife knew all about the work. She had been shocked at first, but had succumbed to the circumstances when she had been forced to choose between a few days away in Blackpool and a luxury holiday in Barbados. She never asked any questions after that.

Morgan never shared his other life with anyone at work; the consequences could be dire. Even more so as he had sometimes received photographs from colleagues who had answered his online advert looking for participants in his movies; of course, none that he'd accepted.

When he started working offshore, he had noticed that the market for the movies was huge. He had been brought up in a strict Catholic household with the world of porn an *alien* to him until he arrived offshore. He saw it as a moneymaking opportunity and had made a great success of it.

Should He Share His Secret...?

Patrick was doing his rounds.

He had been an OIM for many years, the last six on this rig. He lived alone with two cats and a dog. He hated putting them in kennels but that was just how it was. His wife had walked out on him several years ago, fed up with his ambition and his dedication to the job. He admitted the job came first and in all honesty he was glad to see the back of her.

Fortunately, there were no children involved. The only relationship he'd had since then was a couple of shags with Maryanne. No ties, he liked that. He was 52 with red hair cropped short. He was fit; using the on-board gym regularly and a daily swim at his local pool kept him trim.

He confidently boasted that he had no uncovered secrets; Patrick's life was an open book.

The only thing that nobody knew about him was that he had joined a dating site a few weeks ago. He didn't have the guts to put a picture up yet, but that was the next step. He had no interest in a steady relationship, just *looking*.

Patrick sat at his desk and opened his emails.

"Crap, crap and more crap," he grumbled. He deleted all the messages except for three from the dating site. He clicked on the first, leaning forward to view the message with curious eyes. He clicked on the profile.

'Mature bisexual male seeks fun and friendship. Financially independent, no ties. Willing to travel. Prefers males but open-minded.' He went to the messages. He liked two of them so he replied.

Patrick had met several people on the site. One had led to a one-night stand with another offshore worker called Mathew who was married but secretly bisexual. They had a lot in common and had met several times since. They were in touch via email. In his mind, as long as he had his casual encounters, that part of his life was sorted, uncomplicated, and no need for people hanging onto his tail. He was now in his 50s and continually frustrated that he was unable to be himself. There was always something he had to hold back on, unable to share.

That's what he hated about being offshore, the testosterone thing, and the 'man's world' attitude. He envied everyone else with their perfect little lives and their heterosexual relationships. He was pig sick of sitting in the galley listening to their suburban perfectness and the trimmings that went with it. He'd had that for a while with his wife and it bored the tits off him. He just wished he could be open about his 'real' life. It might just be a dating site but it was a taboo subject. He only got angry with himself offshore; he never swore at home but out on the rig it was "fuck this" and "fuck that". It seemed that swearing was the only way to get a response from people.

Terry knocked on the door and Patrick called him in.

"How are things with you Patrick? Just coming onto nights, have you a minute for handover?" asked Terry, yawning and plonking himself on the bed.

"Yep, let's do it lad. I'll meet you in your office in a minute," replied Patrick. He turned off his laptop and left the room.

They discussed the day's activities and then Terry fetched some coffee.

"I envy you sometimes Terry. Your great life in Tenerife with Stephanie, it all sounds just perfect. When are you ever going to make an honest woman of her?"

Terry hated lying to Patrick. He had been supportive of the time off that Terry had needed when he and Stephan were having a hard time in their old house. He had told him that the problem involved difficult neighbours.

Terry felt uncomfortable in his seat. He blushed at Patrick's remarks and laughed off the comment. He *wanted* to be honest with Patrick.

A few days passed and it was eventually time to go home. The atmosphere had picked up. The drill crew changed on a Monday, the maintenance crew and the medic on a Tuesday, and Terry and Patrick on a Wednesday. Alec needed to stay on a few days to cover sickness. Some story from his 'dick of a relief' about another granny dying.

"He must have some amount of relatives. He goes to more funerals than a hearse!" Alec joked with Terry and Patrick as they left for the helicopter. Alec didn't mind – his son could wait another 48 hours.

The bar in the hotel was always a great place to be in the evening. Crew change was at 9pm so almost all the passengers stayed in the hotel at the heliport. Maryanne had chosen her victim. She sat at the bar in her short black skirt and low-cut tight top. She looked good for her age. She had a service hand from Inverness with her, stuck in her little trap like a fly in a spider's web. Terry gave them a wave as he passed by to go to the loo. They had gone by the time he came back.

Patrick got the beers in and went to sit with Terry. It had been a while since they had chatted out of work. Terry would often go into town with Alec, so this was a rare chance to talk.

Patrick was always comfortable with Terry, as a friend and as his manager.

"I really need to tell you something, something that nobody knows Terry. I hate lying to you, so here it is. If you cannot handle it, then I understand." Terry pulled his seat closer to the table, putting his fists under his chin, leaning forward. He listened.

Patrick could see his eyes wanting and dilated. He was curious.

"Well, it's my sexuality. I joined a dating agency about a year ago and I've found I prefer males to females." He watched for a reaction.

"Patrick my friend," said Terry, "I feel humbled and grateful that you feel you can share that with me." He leaned over the table and placed both hands on Patrick's shoulders. "It's fine, really it is," Terry assured him.

Patrick felt elated. He had never realised that it was so easy to share his feelings with people, he could never do that with his ex, she would mock him even if he cried at a sad movie, so he told her nothing.

Terry wanted to tell Patrick of *his* secret life, but not now, this was Patrick's moment. They had a good night and agreed that Patrick should book a trip to Tenerife as soon as possible.

Alec was tired he wanted to go home.

"Look, you ungrateful cow, I need to stay on to cover. I'll be home in two days, that's just the way it is!" shouted Alec across the desk to his hands free phone. His wife's voice screeched back across the room – even the lights flickered at her tone, as if a poltergeist had just come in.

"Typical! You selfish sod. The one night I wanted to go out and give my mum a break from babysitting and you're not here. Just piss off and stay on your stupid rig," came Katrina's angry response. The sudden change in ringtone as she slammed the receiver down was music to Alec's ears.

She was gone.

Katrina texted her friend Lesley and apologised for cancelling their evening in town. She was disappointed; she loved to go out but her mum had bingo tonight so she had no choice but to cancel. She opened a bottle of white wine, poured a glass and sat at the computer, scanning the dating sites and updating her profile on the ones she was a member of.

Alec lay in his cabin. The cream plastic walls were bare of pictures and he could touch the little toilet door at the far end of his bed with his toes. The TV picture was fuzzy but he was happy.

He would see his little Joshua tomorrow.

It was peaceful in his little cabin. He fell asleep.

Nothing is for Ever...

Katrina fell onto the sofa, her eyes hurt, her head pounded. If she had been stopped on the school run by the police she was sure she would have had a positive breath test. She poured a coffee and went back to bed.

Alec and two other passengers waited in the heli lounge. Steven gave them the briefing.

"Enjoy your time off lads," smiled Steven as he watched the three men make their way to the helicopter. It was windy but just below the level which would prevent flying.

It was not long before the radio operator, a Portuguese lad with a thick accent, seemed to be calling for assistance in the radio room. Steven left the smoke room and made his way up. Patrick's relief was there and so was the tool pusher. The helicopter had ditched twenty miles from the beach. Steven felt his knees buckle under him. *Oh God, Alec.* He didn't know the other two guys; they had only been there to do a few jobs before leaving. They stood listening to the chaos on the radios.

It was two hours later when John the OIM made an announcement. He asked everyone to go to their muster stations; it was not a drill, nor was it an emergency. Once the head count had been completed, he visited both stations and confirmed the news that the three passengers and two crew were missing. He'd been crying. Grown men sobbed. Alec was well-known; the other four guys had family too. The rig was devastated.

48

Katrina lay with her head on the pillow, her saliva sticking to the material. She got up and sat on the end of the bed.

"Christ, I'd better make an effort, he'll be home soon," she said to the dog that was sitting looking at her with his legs crossed. She opened the door and let the dog out. It was windy. She showered and dressed. She was sat watching *Loose Women* when there was a knock at the door. It was Cynthia from the house opposite.

"Come on in, want a cuppa?" asked Katrina as she looked over her shoulder at Cynthia following her into the kitchen.

"Have you seen the news Katrina?" She stopped Katrina from filling the kettle. "Katrina, a chopper has gone down."

"Oh, Alec left earlier this morning. He was going into the office to do some paperwork." She felt uncomfortable with Cynthia's look.

"What is it? What?" asked Katrina. Cynthia changed the channel on the TV.

There it was, all over the screen. It was Alec's rig. She knew he would be okay; he was the ever-perfect man, always in the right place at the right time.

Cynthia told her to call the number displayed on the screen to put her mind at rest.

As Katrina went over to the little nest of tables next to the window where the phone sat, she saw them. Two police officers coming up the drive. She stood and watched as they came to the door.

She never heard the bell.

Terry loved the feel of the warm air on his face as he left the plane. It was a great feeling arriving in the Canaries winter with the sun in the sky and the smell of the Mediterranean in the air.

He was keen to tell Stephen of Patrick's revelations; it was like running home from school to tell his dad he was in the school football team. He passed the carousel, having only hand luggage, and made his way to arrivals. He was surprised to see Stephen standing at the back against the glass door, he was normally at the front, waving.

The hall was busy, three flights landing at the same time. Terry was confused at Stephen's expression. He looked worried. He gave Stephen a hug.

"What's the matter? You look like someone just died." Said Terry.

Stephen stared into his eyes, looking terrified.

"Oh God, not your mum, oh Stephen." He went to hug him. Stephen pushed him back and held his forearms tightly.

"I don't know how to tell you this. A helicopter went down this morning. Alec was on it." Terry tilted his head and looked at Stephen.

"Was it from my rig?"

"Yes, it was."

"Christ, how many were on it?"

"Five, three passengers and two crew," replied Stephen, watching Terry closely. Terry took his phone from his bag.

"I'm just going to phone Alec and get an update." He was shaking. "The news coverage in Aberdeen will be bang up to date." Stephen put his hand out to stop him dialling the number.

"Terry, Alec is dead, he was on the helicopter." Stephen felt his own tears welling in his eyes. Terry kept looking at the phone; he twitched a few times, put the phone in his pocket and walked towards the exit. Stephen picked up a jogging pace to keep up with him.

In the fresh air, Terry fell to his knees and wept.

Katrina trundled along in the coming days. Her mum was in charge. Joshua stayed in his room under the protective eye of her parents.

She sat looking into the mirror the evening before the funeral. Her reflection looked tired and confused. Her husband and provider were dead. She was a widow at 46. She pushed the skin up below her eyes. *A facelift is in order once the insurance is sorted,* she thought.

Joshua was at her mum's; Katrina accepted that he was closer to her parents than he was to her. She looked at the little red clock and the marks on the wall. She picked up the clock and put it in the bottom drawer then went to the kitchen for a cloth and wiped the wall clean. It was half past ten; the house was empty for the first time in days.

The funeral was tomorrow.

She went to the little bar that Alec had made in the conservatory. She took a bottle off the shelf and filled her glass. She drank herself to sleep.

"My house, my postcode," she muttered to herself as she drifted off.

Terry sat with Patrick towards the back of church. Neither had met Katrina. She was certainly just as Alec had described. She sailed into church dragging the little boy with her in his school uniform. Her mum and dad were close behind, seemingly with more of an eye on the little boy than their widowed daughter. She was dressed in black with a hat more fitting for an episode of *Big Fat Gypsy Weddings*. Terry raised his eyes in disbelief as he looked at her face covered by a black veil.

"Jesus, Patrick, the black widow. What the hell does she look like?" Patrick tried to keep his laughter in; there were several rows of people behind them.

"I think she's pissed," replied Patrick. It was hard for her to cover that up. After all, a bottle of gin in two hours was catching up with her metabolism.

The graveside was even more farcical.

As the minister offered her some soil to throw onto the coffin, she hesitated and then asked around for a glove. In disgust, her dad thrust his towards her. She put the glove on and accepted the soil. It was pathetic. Terry felt the pain of little Joshua, his wide eyes staring at the box in the hole. *It must be so confusing for him,* he thought. His grandparents stood protectively by the little boy's side. Katrina turned and made her way to the car in a move that could have come straight from *Gone with the Wind*, her hand on her forehead and the other with a handkerchief at her nose. She stopped halfway to the car, making sure the 'media' at the main gate of the cemetery got a good view of her in her *mourning glory*.

She went scurrying back for her left luggage – little Joshua. She wandered around looking for him. He had already left with his grandparents.

"Fuck him," she said. She sat in the back of the car, opened her hip flask and slugged a few mouthfuls of gin.

The months that followed on the rig were difficult.

People talked of their fond memories of Alec. At times, Terry felt like he'd lost his partner; the looks of sympathy were claustrophobic.

At teatimes, he would socialise, feeling Alec's name was always avoided. He felt he wanted to stand up some days in the galley and shout, "He's dead. I know, let's just move on."

He never did.

Randy Wee Rancoon

Morgan Pearson sat in the lounge of the airport. He was a small man, about 5ft 4in. He had a stubbly beard, lighter than his red hair, his blue eyes were hidden by his sunglasses. He never wore designer clothes, but looked smart in a selection of 'superstore 'labels, easily passing as a man in his late 40s with probably a professional career. He had his camera case beside him. He drank the wine that was free in the lounge and scanned the room. It was almost empty. He liked flying first class, even if it was just to London from Aberdeen.

He had arranged to meet his business partner Lenny at a hotel they used regularly for filming. They had some auditions that evening. He always found them interesting.

They had planned a 'screw my wife' movie. They seemed to be popular at the moment. He was amazed at the response to his online and newspaper adverts; they'd had over eight hundred couples apply. They had worked the number down to twenty and were looking for twelve couples to film. One movie a month would be released next year.

The hotel was smart, not plush, but enough to give an air of professionalism. The staff on reception couldn't care less what his business was. He had booked the small conference suite for two days and had paid in advance. What they did behind the door was their business. Morgan had registered the use as 'interviews for his company.' Never in a million years would anyone looking at him think he was the director of a pornography company.

Lenny was already in the room, setting up the equipment. It was a bright room with a glass roof, no windows, the door locked from within. There was a long table with four chairs behind it at one end and opposite there was a blue sofa, comfortably big enough for three people, and firm so those being interviewed did not disappear down the back of the cushions.

"Hey Lenny, good to see you," said Morgan.

"All good Morgan, the first couple will be here in ten minutes. They just texted to say they were in the car park," replied Lenny.

"Okay, let's get going then, lots to do."

The little grey phone on the wall rang. Lenny picked up the receiver.

"That's the first couple at reception; I'll go get them," he said leaving the room.

Morgan sat on the desk, looking casual; he had done this for twelve years. The couple looked like their picture which was always a bonus; better than a picture of someone in their twenties and then a 60-year-old turns up with her fanny prolapsed at the knees or her tits big enough to go over her shoulder and slap her bum. Morgan had seen it all.

The woman did the talking. She was a brunette, about 5ft 8in, fit and confident. He was a little taller, cropped dark hair, clean-shaven and a regular at the gym. Morgan asked the usual questions, why they wanted to be filmed, had they done this before and did they have a previous contract with other companies.

The woman stripped off easily for the camera, he was a bit more hesitant, as most blokes were. They were booked. One couple done. The next ones were all suitable and the bookings were made.

That evening, they began the filming. Morgan never got excited; he actually found it all a bit distasteful as two couples watched each other have sex with their partners across the room. Lenny played with himself on occasions.

Lenny enjoyed the change in filming, he was a professional photographer, normally doing wedding and portraits .He found this exciting.

Morgan was pissed off with one woman who had wet herself on the floor, staining the carpet. He hated that, his credit card would be charged. She apologised and even seemed embarrassed. *Jeez,* thought Morgan, *you shag someone you don't know for an hour in front of your husband, but get embarrassed when you pish on the carpet.* He never stopped being amazed at people.

He was soon back at the airport and heading home, new movies ready to sell on line.

The three weeks off passed quickly.

The heliport was busy as usual for early check-in. He sat next to Maryanne.

"How was your time off Morgan, get up to much?" she asked.

"Na, not much, bit of DIY," he replied. If only she knew. He never really took to Maryanne; he always thought she smelt of sperm.

She had replied to some of his ads a few years ago.

If only she knew.

Reality Kicks In On The beach...

It had been four months since Alec had died. Katrina reluctantly agreed to meet with Jessica. She still saw her every morning at the bus stop.

She was still waiting for the finances to be settled. She had great plans to extend the house, new car.

The two women hugged awkwardly in the café at the superstore.

Katrina had her hair loose, now dyed brown, with her big brown sunglasses sitting on top of her head. Her heels and dress matched, as always. Jessica sat opposite her on one the little sofas with the coffee table between them. She had her trusted jeans on and a plain white blouse. She wore no make-up but to anyone passing she was much more attractive than Katrina. The waitress came and took their orders.

"How are you these days? You look well, I admire your courage," said Jessica as she 'doe-eyed' Katrina.

"Oh, I cope Jessica. The pain is still there but I've got Joshua to help me through."

She flicked her hair and fluttered her eyes in a pathetic effort to look forlorn.

"I had seventeen wonderful years with Alec. I have those memories in my heart," she gushed.

Oh hells bells Katrina, thought Jessica, *that's a well-used speech. I heard you say that to people at the funeral.*

"Oh, I know Katrina," she replied, trying not to laugh. "Maybe when things get better you will find someone else," suggested Jessica, giving her a sympathetic smile.

"Oh no Jessica, I couldn't imagine going with someone else. Alec was the love of my life."

Jessica thought she would choke on her coffee as she watched Katrina and listened with her cup at her mouth.

"At least you have no money worries which was the worst thing when Tom left me. I had nothing, he might as well have been dead."

Katrina took her compact mirror out and checked her face.

"Oh I know, it must be so hard. I could never wear supermarket clothes, and the thought of Joshua going to a state school, all those working classes, fighting and all."

Jessica wanted to throw her coffee over her and tell her what she knew. *Yes, you dirty old slag end of a slut, shagging around in a hotel like a cheap prostitute.* But she didn't.

The women continued their conversation before saying their goodbyes. Katrina strutted to her car and drove off. Jessica went to the toilet to compose herself.

Katrina didn't recognise the car in her drive. A silver Mercedes. She parked next to it. She walked to the driver's side. A middle-aged man in a pinstriped suit opened the door and got out.

"Brian Parton, I don't think we've met Mrs Young." She accepted his gesture and shook his hand. "I'm Alec's accountant. I did try to call you and I wrote a couple of letters." Katrina was flustered.

"Oh, of course, I've been so busy, I meant to call you. Please come in." She did her usual pathetic flirt and trotted to the front door. Brian had known Alec for many years, managing his taxes and investments. They sat opposite each other in the sitting room. Katrina scanned her visitor. He was tall and slim, salt and pepper hair, cropped and tidy. His suit was expensive and so was his smell. His wedding ring seemed old, settled and content.

"Well, Mrs Young, we have a few things to discuss. Did Alec ever share the contents of his will with you?" He looked carefully at her, knowing full well that he hadn't or she would have left Alec several years ago. He waited for a reply. His blue, almost grey eyes were making Katrina a little uncomfortable.

"No, never. Alec did all the bills and that sort of stuff. He transferred funds to me every month and that worked well," she replied, feeling a bit dim, if not even totally thick.

"I have the will here. I'm afraid you are not going to be happy Mrs Young. Alec left everything to Joshua, in trust until he is 21 and cited your parents as governors of the funds. In the case of their death, his friend Terry will oversee matters."

"What the fuck do you mean?" retorted Katrina. "We were married for seventeen years so surely I'm entitled to something." She stood up and began to pace the floor. "He cannot do this, we both bought this house."

Brian changed position, moving forward on the sofa. He'd expected this.

"Well, Mrs Young, you are not on the mortgage, the house was in your husband's name only, as are his shares and investments, and there is nothing in your name at all."

Katrina bit her bottom lip. She was breathing heavily. Brian knew it was time to leave. He put a copy of the documents on the coffee table.

"I'll show myself out, my card is with the documents, call me if you have any questions."

Katrina ignored him; she jumped at the sound of the door closing. She went to the fridge and opened a bottle of wine.

"Stuff the glass," she exclaimed and drank from the bottle. She went into the sitting room and scanned the papers. Everything was Josh's.

She kicked the table over and threw the wine bottle against the wall. She looked up at the ceiling.

"Yes, you sod, bet you're laughing your head off up there." She screamed and stomped, then fell onto the sofa sobbing.

Dirty Bitch....

Maryanne was in her office. She had three days left on the rig.

Her mother still phoned her four times a day when she was at work. She hadn't objected to it initially, she worried about her. The nursing staff tried to occupy her mother in different ways when she asked to phone, but Maryanne knew that it was a thankless task for someone with dementia.

She still got upset when she went to visit her in the nursing home. She had gone to her mother's room on one occasion while the nursing staff went to fetch her from the garden. Maryanne was busy putting some new clothes in the wardrobe when her mother had come into the room and screamed that there was a burglar in her house. She had picked up a lamp and threw it at Maryanne, narrowly missing her head.

Sometimes, Maryanne would look at her mother and she would get butterflies in her stomach, hoping that she might recognise her, but that was soon dashed when she began to ask who she was and what she wanted. She had taken her mother out of the nursing home some months ago as she hated seeing her upset. She cared for her when she was at home. When she was at work, she had a live-in carer.

This trip had been quiet. She was on the computer when Patrick popped his head around the door of the rig hospital. She liked Patrick. They had similar lives, so she thought.

"Coffee or tea," he asked.

"Coffee would be perfect," she replied. He soon returned, shutting the door behind him. It was 11pm, neither of them could sleep.

Patrick was keeping out of the way of the night tool pusher, Maryanne was on *Facebook*. She sat in a little lace top she wore to bed and her tight shorts. She swung around to face Patrick. He could see her breasts through the top, the light from the table lamp making them more visible. She knew he was looking at them. She sipped her coffee and gave him a wink.

"Been to the gym then?" she asked. "You look flushed."

"No, I went for a run on the Heli Deck." His blue T-shirt stuck to his skin, his grey tracksuit bottoms were stained with sweat.

She slipped off her flip-flops and rubbed her foot against his leg, watching him as she held the cup in both hands, sipping her coffee. He leaned over and put his hand inside her blouse. She put the coffee on the table, placing her hands behind her head. The hospital was a bright room with good lighting. There was four hospital beds at one end with white cupboards and shelves on the walls. The entrance to the corridor was behind where Patrick sat. Behind Maryanne was the door to her cabin. Patrick lifted her blouse over her head. She edged forward to allow him to take off her shorts. He leaned over and kissed her.

Maryanne wrapped her legs around his waist, taking his top off. He slipped inside her. She laughed as she moved back and forward in her chair.

Without leaving her gaze, he picked her up and walked into the cabin, kicking the door closed behind him.

Dick On A Stick...

The neighbours avoided her.

It was dark before Katrina would leave the house.

Normally, she was not sober enough to drive the car until late morning. Joshua was now with his grandparents during the week. The private school had given notice that he would have to leave once she fell behind with the fees. She scoffed at her mum when she told her that Josh was flourishing in the local primary near their house.

"He seems like a different boy, even with the pain of losing his father, he seems to be mixing well and fitting in," said her mum over the phone. Her mum was clever; she had worked in a bank until she retired and looked after her health and that of Katrina's dad. They both looked younger than their 68 years.

Her dad had rarely spoken to her in recent months, embarrassed at her drinking and the neglect of her son. "You stupid cow, pull yourself together and get a grip. You still have Joshua to think of," he had shouted at her one morning after using the spare key to let himself in. She had been asleep at the bottom of the stairs, an empty bottle of gin at her side and vomit on the bottom stair. She vaguely remembered seeing his shoes as she opened her eyes, his voice distant but recognisable, and then the door banging.

Katrina got into the car.

"Oh Christ, look at me," she groaned as she focused the mirror on her face. "Need to get my roots done." She flicked her fingers through her hair, ignoring the moving curtains from the neighbours. "Fuck off," she shouted with the car window still shut. She spun her wheels as she left the driveway. A rebellious screech.

She had two days left in her beloved postcode. The house had been repossessed by the bank. The council had given her a flat in the city on the tenth floor of a high-rise block which she accepted without viewing. She had no choice.

Stephen was in the Arrivals Lounge, back in his normal place at the front of the line waiting for Terry.

He was going to ask him this time.

He had decided that Terry could stuff his job and his offshore 'Narnia-closeted' crew; he was going to ask him to marry him. Alec's death had made them rethink their lives; life was too short to be uneventful.

The airport was busy.

Tourists piled in through the door, throwing their milk bottle skin at the Mediterranean sky as if it was the last day the sun would ever shine.

Stephen stood waiting.

He wondered what on earth people thought they looked like in their cheap clothes stuck to their overweight bodies, strutting through the airport like they should be on TV.

He had noticed that Terry's flight had landed. He pushed forward to the front of the crowds in Arrivals. He felt good in his black leather trousers and white cotton shirt. He had a bunch of helium balloons in one hand, the ring in the other.

He saw Terry's silhouette emerging. He went down on one knee and pulled out the box with the ring in it.

This caused great interest amongst the crowd, most with one eye searching for the unsuspecting incoming passenger they were waiting for and the other on the overdressed bloke bent down on one knee in an airport.

Stephen was smiling at the surprised look on Terry's face. He knew he could be shy and that's probably why he had put his sunglasses on when he spotted Stephen. Terry walked towards Stephen, hitting him with his bag as he strolled past, sending him sprawling across the floor and scrambling to find the ring. The balloons appeared to shoot off as fast as they could to the glass dome above, seemingly relieved to be free from the ridiculous scene below.

Stephen clambered to his feet.

"Terry, wait. It's me, wait!" He shouted after him. He quickened his pace to catch up. Terry was standing by the car, his arms folded, leaning against the bonnet.

He lifted his glasses.

"What the fuck was that about? You dick on a stick, what was all that pish in there?" He pointed to the airport.

Stephen never got a chance to answer; Terry grabbed the keys out of his hand and got into the car.

"You might be all pink high heels and gay pride flags, but I'm not like that. I'm so far back in the Narnia closet I need satnav to get out!" He was shouting at Stephen. "That's the way I am, so don't ever embarrass me like that again, and get some day clothes, you look like a fucking pimp in that outfit." Stephen knew when to stay quiet. He said nothing.

"I'm surprised some fat tart coming though Arrivals never took the ring and dragged you up the aisle – would have served you right, you twat."

They pulled into the driveway.

Stephen took a deep breath.

"I've booked a table for us at the new Thai restaurant in town tonight," he said quickly.

"Fuck off and go yourself, I'm going to bed," replied Terry. He grabbed his bag and went into the house slamming the door behind him.

Stephen sat half out of the car, watching the ripples on the swimming pool as the evening breeze caught the surface of the water, as if lapping at his feet in sympathy.

The dog came to sit at his feet.

"Well, that was a disaster. No pink collar or wedding poncho for you," he said, tickling the dog's ear.

Things Are Never As They May Seem...

Maryanne pulled into the drive. The house looked quiet.

She had a carer who looked after her mother when she was offshore. Her mother was 61 and had been diagnosed with dementia about three years earlier. Maryanne had known long before the official diagnosis; twenty-three years as a staff nurse had given her more than enough experience to see the signs. Her mother thought she was just forgetful. Maryanne thought it best to let her think that without upsetting her. She had moments when she was as normal as any other woman and other days she had no idea who her daughter was. That upset Maryanne the most.

She never knew her father. It had always been just the two of them. Her mother had been thrown out of the family home when she was pregnant with her. She had succeeded in keeping her baby when many were given up for adoption. She struggled but survived.

Maryanne sat in her little MG convertible looking up at the tidy semi-detached house her mother had worked so hard to buy. The house where Maryanne had lived all her life.

It was not her ideal location now she was an adult. She would have liked a trendy apartment in Aberdeen; she was fed up with commuting. She had few friends in Surrey. Most of her acquaintances had children and had moved on into other circles; new chapters in their lives had opened that Maryanne was not part of.

The carer had left at 9pm once she had confirmed that Maryanne's flight had landed and that she had picked up her car.

She was grateful for the carer being so good. She was in her 40s, a similar age to Maryanne so they had things in common. She had given up work as a carer in an old folk's home to take the job looking after Maryanne's mother. She had been the fourth carer in the post but fortunately her mother had taken to her. That was a big relief for Maryanne.

She quietly opened the door, checked her mother was in bed and went back downstairs.

She was watching the news on the sofa with a glass of wine. She heard the familiar creak of the floorboards upstairs (she knew every creak and groan in this house), listened as the toilet flushed, then sat forward as the footsteps headed to the landing, not back to the bedroom.

She put her glass down and went into the hall. Her mother was halfway down the stairs in her nightie.

"Hello Mother! I got home about an hour ago, you were fast asleep," she said with a smile.

"Get out of my house! Who the hell are you? Get out! Get out!" came the response. Her mother looked angry, her soft face edged with tiredness and confusion.

She was a short, well-kept lady, her silver hair cut in a smart bob, her nails manicured. Maryanne stepped back. She could see the distant look in her mother's eyes.

"Mother, it's me, your daughter Maryanne. I'm home from work to look after you." Her mother had her right hand on the railing, in her other hand she had a baseball bat that Maryanne kept next to her bed, something her mother had always done in case of intruders. Maryanne had taken the bat to her own room after her mother became ill.

"Get out of my house you thieving bitch! I'll get my father up, he'll sort you out."

Maryanne was scared inside but tried to stay calm on the surface; she had never seen her mother this bad. She glanced at the red spot on the carpet.

"Mother, your foot is bleeding. What happened?" she asked.

Her mother let go of the rail and lifted her nightie to look at her foot. She stumbled backwards. Maryanne leaned forward to catch her but as she moved to help she was totally unprepared for the full thrust of the baseball bat that came from her mother's other hand, smacking her across the head and sending her to the floor.

Her mother stepped over the crumpled body at the bottom of the stairs, opened the front door and left the house in her bare feet, slamming the door behind her as she left.

Maryanne felt the room spin, the pain in her head made her nauseous. She remembered what had happened.

She only felt pain in her head; her limbs were okay, stiff from the fall, but she could move them. She crawled to her handbag that was by the front door . She couldn't lift her head as the pain was so intense. She managed to find her mobile and dialled 999. She used all her strength to reach up and open the door, leaving it slightly ajar for access.

She fell unconscious.

Dealing With Change...

The smell was familiar; she knew she was in hospital. She was lying flat on her back on a bed, not on a trolley. *Christ, I've passed through Accident and Emergency. I must have been out of it for ages*, she thought.

She was in a single room; the light on the ceiling hurt her eyes. She tried to turn her head but the pain was intense. It felt as if someone was standing on her face, pushing down on her nose. The pressure was hideous.

"Hi Maryanne, how are you feeling? Good to see you awake," came a soft voice. She opened her eyes and saw the nurse standing by the bed. The white tunic and red epaulettes were familiar. Her blonde hair was tied up on her head. She looked like a typical well-used NHS nurse, meaningful but tired and overworked.

"Hello. My head is awful. How long have I been here?" asked Maryanne.

"Two days. It's been two days. I think maybe you should have some painkillers for that head; you have fourteen stitches in there. It was quite a cut you had," said the nurse

. Maryanne shut her eyes as the nurse disappeared from the room.

"Here you go, take these with this water, they'll help," said the nurse. She helped to prop Maryanne's head forward and she swallowed the tablets.

"My mother. What about my mother? Do you know where she is?" asked Maryanne in a panic.

"I'll get the doctor to come and have a chat. Let the painkillers work, you'll be able to concentrate better once the pain has gone."

She was not sure how long she had been asleep but the pain had disappeared yet there was still a distant throb as the painkillers battled to keep the headache at bay.

"Hello Maryanne, long time no see. It's Martin Heart. Remember me from Ward E5?"

Dr Heart had worked with Maryanne before she had left to go offshore; they had been good friends at work, nothing else.

She felt his hands take hold of her right hand which was resting on the bed. She felt the wedding ring missing from his finger against her knuckle. She remembered that he had *never* taken the ring off when she had worked with him.

"Hi Martin, good to see you. I'm looking my best, especially for you!" They both chuckled politely.

Martin Heart was a heavyset man with broad shoulders. He always had an afternoon shadow of a beard and he often joked that it was standard NHS issue. Many of the female staff were gutted when he married one of the girls from the staff canteen. He had been one of the most eligible bachelors in Maryanne's day. Not her type, but she did find it amusing to see her colleagues wet their panties when he came onto the ward.

"That's some bashing you got on your head lady," he said.

"Well, I will try and steal old lady's handbags in the street," she replied, moving her head to look at his face. He still had those piercing blue eyes and his bedside manner was always superb – calming and reassuring.

"My mother Martin, do you know anything about her? I have no idea what happened after the fall. I remember making the call and leaving the door ajar for the ambulance crew but that's about it." She looked at Martin without moving her head. She felt sick to the pit of her stomach. "Is she okay? Please tell me."

"She's safe Maryanne. I went over to St Richard's Nursing Home this morning to check on her. She was picked up by the police in the shopping precinct along the road from your house. She was cold, but otherwise she's fine. She was asking for you. She said she thought you would have been home by now."

Maryanne felt the tears push through. She tried to hold them back but they were winning, like a tsunami flooding over the man-made walls built to prevent an overflow. She didn't want to cry; she knew any movement would be painful.

"Maryanne, you need to rest. You will feel much better in a day or two. Your mother is safe so you need to focus on getting better."

Martin sat with her until she fell asleep. He kissed her on the forehead and left.

Martin had split with his wife two years earlier. He had wanted children, she had not. They'd been happy for a few years; she had given up her job in a canteen and had gone to college, eventually managing to fulfil her ambition of becoming a primary school teacher, thanks to Martin funding her studies. He had no bitterness; he was glad she was happy in her career.

He had come home early one evening and caught her in bed with a colleague she worked with. A female colleague. There was no shouting or fighting. He packed his stuff and left. The divorce was amicable, she had moved on. He was just where he had always been for thirteen or fourteen hours a day – in the hospital.

Martin pulled the collar of his white jacket up as he left the building and made his way to his car. It was cold, or he was overtired, he was not sure which. He opened the boot of his car and threw his white jacket in. It landed on the pile that was already there – *weeks' worth,* he thought. He got in the car and left.

He smiled as he thought of Maryanne.

Risky Money Making....

She had to take the bus. She had no car.

Her dad had arranged for the delivery of her furniture and possessions.

Katrina sat with her face against the window, the rain hitting the glass as she travelled in and out of the Aberdeen suburbs that she had never known.

She got off the bus and looked up at the high-rise flats. There was a group of women standing at the entrance to the block, smoking and chatting. They glanced uninterestingly at Katrina. She looked tired and worn having slept in a bed and breakfast for the last few days.

She ignored the women and went into the foyer. She waited for the lift. An elderly man came wobbling out, looking at the floor as he passed her, the smell of urine was overpowering. Katrina pressed the button for the 10th floor.

She had not seen the flat.

There were eight doors on either side of the landing, all green; some looked more cared for than others. Number 110 was at the end. She fumbled in her bag for the key. It was musty inside. Her belongings were piled high in each room. There were no carpets, just linoleum. The cramped hall had four doors leading off it. There was a small bedroom, a kitchen and a bathroom and at the entrance at the end of the hall there was a living room with a glass door leading to a balcony.

Katrina sat on the sofa that was covered in plastic and wept.

She had lost her postcode and her provider. She had been sacked from her job at the garage for smelling of alcohol at work. She would get £53 per week dole money and that was all.

She needed to sort herself out.

She took off her jacket and shoes and began to unpack.

She watched the sun go down from her balcony and she listened to the shouting and swearing from some of the other flats. She had a gin in one hand and a fag in the other.

She needed some more drink. She took her purse and emptied out the last coins onto the little table. Not even enough for a Mars bar. She threw her purse across the room.

She put on some make-up and left.

The streets were quiet. Katrina wandered a while.

It was not long before a car pulled up. The man in the driver's seat lowered the window at the passenger side.

"You looking for a few bob girl?" he asked.

She stopped and looked in. He was a fat man with a beard.

"Yes I am," she replied.

"Get in then," he said leaning over and unlocking the door.

They drove a short way without speaking. He told her to get into the back of the car. He gave her three £10 notes.

She got out, took her knickers off and lay on the back seat. She shut her eyes as his saliva dripped on her face, his belly crushing her abdomen. She never gave a passing care about using protection. She was as low as she could get.

She just needed to make money.

He dropped her off and asked for her mobile number. *My first client,* she thought.

She bought some gin and went back to her flat.

In the weeks that followed, Katrina joined an escort agency. She began to build up her clients. She bought some new clothes, had a manicure and got her roots done.

She examined her reflection in the mirror one evening as she was getting ready to go out.

"Hello prostitute," she said. She didn't care. She would do what she had to in order to get her postcode back.

The Pain Of Dementia...

Maryanne disliked these places.

She stood looking up at the purpose-built, modern building.

The sign above the door – St Richard's Care Home – was weather-worn. The building looked tired.

She thought the charges for beds in these places were ludicrous and even more awful was how the funding was arranged. If her mother owned her house she would have to meet the full cost of her care, even if it meant selling the property to fund it whereas if her mother had nothing, she would still be entitled to the same care, but it would be government-funded.

Her mother had been wise enough to sign her house over to Maryanne many years ago, so that if she ever needed care then she wouldn't have to sell the house to pay for it. Maryanne smiled as she remembered the day the house was signed over to her. She had just graduated from nursing school .Her pals got fob watches and stethoscopes as gifts – she got a house! In her mind, it was always "theirs" but she was pleased her mother was wise enough to have planned ahead.

The smell of urine shot up her nostrils. Not a fresh smell, but a bleached, diluted odour, a vain attempt to disguise the stench. A young carer, no older than 18, took Maryanne to the lounge where her mother was sitting. She had to scan the room to find her. She was sitting in the alcove near the window reading a paper.

"Hi Mother, how are you?" she asked, kneeling down next to the seat.

"Oh my darling girl, you're home. I've been so worried. Where have you been? I thought one of those helicopters had crashed and that's why I had been put in here. No one tells me anything these days."

She stood up and pulled her daughter close. Maryanne thought she would cry. She cherished these very rare hugs from her mother, a really meaningful mother's embrace.

"Oh, I just got held up at work, weather and all that."

"You've had your hair done, all piled up in a bun. That's pretty."

"Yes, just fancied a change."

She did not want to lie but sometimes that was the best thing to do. Her hair had been shaved on the right side where the stitches were so the hairdresser had put extensions in and arranged her hair to cover the bald patch.

"When can I come home Maryanne? I'm already packed."

Maryanne looked at her mother's pleading eyes, her stomach felt as if someone was inside poking at her with a knife.

"What on earth have you got on Mother? I've never seen you in that before." She looked at the label on the inside of the neck. "I'll be back in a minute."

At the end of the corridor, she could see a well-dressed woman with staff hovering around her.

"Like flies around shite," said Maryanne under her breath.

"Hi, are you the manager?" asked Maryanne politely.

"Yes, Rachel Monique, can I help you?"

"Oh, I hope you can. My mother is Annette Jacobs, she came in last week."

"Oh, I see. You're the high-flying offshore daughter she talks about? The one she hit with a baseball bat?"

One of the younger members of staff giggled at the comment but soon changed her expression on receipt of an angry stare from Maryanne.

"Can you tell me why my mother is wearing someone else's clothes and why she smells of piss? She is not incontinent and there is a urine stain on the seat." She noticed the manager's uncomfortable shuffle and she looked at the three girls standing listening to the conversation.

One of them stepped forward; she looked to be oldest of the three.

"I put Annie in that seat this morning but I never noticed the wet chair under after she had sat down. I took her back and changed her into the clothes that were in her wardrobe."

Maryanne felt the fire in her belly. She glowered at the manager who was now sweating.

"Her name is Annette, not fucking Annie, you stupid woman. I expect some idiot on nights has put the wrong clothes in her wardrobe. Let's hope she got the correct medication during the drug round," said Maryanne in a quiet but angry voice.

The three carers were looking uneasy, changing position and glancing at each other, not really knowing what to do.

Maryanne turned her attention to the manager.

"As for you, I want you – no one else –to get my mother ready to go immediately. Whilst you are doing that I will be making a call to the Care Commission to tell them what a filthy hole you manage here."

She turned and walked back to where her mother was.

"Come on Mother, let's get you home."

"I am home dear. I know your face, do you work with my dad?" asked her mother.

The manager came in and avoided eye contact with Maryanne who waited for her mother in reception. No words were exchanged.

Maryanne took her mother home. She never phoned the Care Commission; there was nothing unusual about what had happened. She would read about this in the papers every week. She had seen it many times before.

The live in carer was called Josephine. It had been three weeks since Maryanne's accident, one week of her time off had been spend in hospital.

Josephine had popped round the evening before Maryanne was leaving for work.

"Bloody hells bells Maryanne, she could have killed you." She gave Maryanne a hug and then took off her coat.

"Do you want a drink Josephine?"

"Oh go on then, a brandy. My husband is picking me up in an hour."

The women chatted about Annette. "You will have to think about a care home soon Maryanne, your mother is hard work. I never tell you everything as I don't want to worry you when you're away."

"I know Josephine, I know." Maryanne put her head in her hands. "I know that it's the best thing to do but it's just making the decision. I'll give it some thought this time at work. I think this episode might be when push comes to shove." The women talked for a while longer.

Josephine hugged Maryanne as she left. "She will be fine with me but you need to think long and hard," she said looking at Maryanne. They bid their farewells.

It was 9am.

Josephine was in the kitchen making Annette's breakfast when the front doorbell rang.

Maryanne answered the door.

"Oh hi Martin, this is a nice surprise." He was standing on the path in a black leather jacket and jeans.

"I'm on my way to work and thought I might give you a lift to the airport; you don't want to be driving that MG next month, it's November, the roads can be bad."

"I know, it's going into hibernation next week, the guy from the garage is picking it up for me. I have a taxi booked for eleven."

"Come on, how about brunch with me and then I'll drop you off at the airport?" She felt a flutter in her stomach. He was still dashingly handsome, his teeth as white as snow.

"Okay, give me five minutes. I'd invite you in but Mother gets confused by strangers." He had already turned heels and was heading back to his shogun.

Maryanne had a quick chat with Josephine and gave her the car keys for the garage man.

"Bye Mother," she said as she knelt down next to Annette at the table.

"Oh yes, thank you very much, you have done a good job dear," replied her mother who then turned to Josephine. "She's a very good cleaner you know; my mother always said 'a good housekeeper is like gold dust'". Maryanne caught Josephine's eye, they both laughed quietly.

She got into the car.

"This is a lovely treat Martin." He was clean-shaven and looked a bit younger without his shadow. His crisp white shirt complemented his tanned skin. "Have you been on holiday?" she asked. "You look tanned."

"Yep, I have, just had a week in Malta. Just sat by the pool, drank and read my books – was a dream," he replied.

"How is Cynthia these days? Any little Martins yet?" asked Maryanne.

He threw her a glance.

"I take it you don't keep in touch with anyone from the hospital then." She changed position to look at him.

"No, why?"

"Well, we were divorced eighteen months ago, long story, but it's all under the bridge now, moved on from that."

She felt the butterflies in her stomach. She tried really hard to stay calm. *Fuck, he's single, oh my God, oh my God.*

"Oh, I am surprised. You always looked really happy together."

"Never mind that Maryanne. We have a few hours, let's get brunch and catch up."

They stopped at a pub near the airport.

They chatted as if they still worked together and knew all about each other's goings-on. He still loved her saucer eyes and her natural flirtatious way; he had always found her attractive.

"Are you seeing anyone then?" he asked as she put the last piece of scampi in her mouth, making him burst out laughing as she pretended to be shocked at his question.

"No, no. Can you imagine me bringing anyone home? My mother would batter them with the bat!" They both laughed.

"Okay, when you're back in three weeks, we'll have a date. I always kind of fancied you and it's time I tried you out."

She kicked him under the table.

"I'm not a bike," she said smiling at him.

"Oh I know that," he replied, "but I do remember you telling me that you loved to try before you buy, and that was just a drink." Maryanne threw her head back with laughter.

"Well okay, a meal it is then when I'm home."

He walked her to the departure gate.

"Let me see that wound before you go, make sure it's healing well." She leaned her head over, letting him part the extensions covering her wound.

"Looks healthy girl. Healing well."

"I'd better go or I'll miss the flight." She leaned forward to kiss him on the cheek but he deliberately moved his head to catch her lips. She hesitated before letting him pull her close.

She felt her knees tremble and the colour rush to her face.

"Sorry Maryanne, hope that wasn't too much." She felt her cheeks burn.

"No Martin, it wasn't enough." She winked at him and blew him a kiss as she headed off through security.

Maryanne sat on the plane looking out the window. Of all the guys she had met in her life, Martin was one of the few she could spend the rest of her days with. They got on well and now they obviously fancied each other. She felt like a teenager with her first boyfriend. She had no space in her life for a relationship but maybe now it was time to make space. Could she break her habit and go home to Martin this trip?

She looked at her reflection in the window. *We'll see.*

Just Too Greedy...

Jessica Linthorpe was finishing her shift at the hotel. The reception area was quiet. She was polishing the mirrors next to the lift when she saw her.

She needed a double take to make sure it was Katrina. Two men were with her. She could hardly walk.

She watched as one of the men went to reception while the other made his way to the lift. She moved silently behind the pillar.

"Oh my God, look at her, she must be on something," she whispered to herself.

She was wearing a tight yellow dress which stopped mid-thigh, white high heels and a cheap white linen jacket.

"The money. I want the money first," said Katrina. "I'm not a whore; I'm a fucking high-class prostitute so pay me first." Her slurred tones echoed around the marble hallway.

Jessica watched, her mouth wide open as one man thrust a pile of notes into her bag.

"You'd better be good you slut," she heard him say.

The other bloke joined them and Jessica watched as they got into the lift.

It was 6am when Jessica came in for her shift; she was shocked at what she had witnessed the previous night. *What the hell had happened to Katrina?* Before she had time to take off her jacket, she saw the two men leave, putting the key on the reception desk. Jessica noted the room number – 354.

She got her trolley and waved briefly to the other woman who was cleaning the bar.

She went to Room 354.

The door was ajar. She pushed it open. It was dark. She walked over to open the curtains but tripped over something.

Katrina was lying face down naked on the floor in a pool of blood. She rolled her over and screamed.

In her mouth was a sock stuffed in so far that the edges of her mouth were torn and bleeding. She had blood coming from other extremities. Her eyes were rolled back in their sockets.

Jessica ran into the hall and down to reception.

The place was soon buzzing with police and paramedics. Jessica sat at reception with the other staff. Her manager comforted her and assured her that she could have some time off to recover. She never told them that she knew the dead woman.

At about half past ten, the lift came down with Katrina's body. The staff watched as the metal trolley trundled through the foyer and down the wheelchair ramp. A few guests looked on from the bar area.

Bigamy...

Brendan Hastings, the driller, sat in his cabin. He was tired. He was going home tomorrow. Home to somewhere ... or someone.

He had been married to his Spanish wife Carona for eight years. They had two girls aged 5 and 3. They had met whilst he was in Malaga on a course; they'd had a 'quickie wedding' in Las Vegas when they were on holiday, much to the horror of her strict Catholic family. They set up home in Malaga. Ideal for the airport and Brendan's travelling.

He had met his 'other wife' Emma long before he married Carona. They came from the same neighbourhood and were married when he was 23. He was now 37. She had wanted a baby for years but they just never seemed to get it together, unlike Carona who would fall pregnant at the fall of a fart.

If he had to choose, he knew it would be Carona. She was dark, sultry and never asked any questions. She was passionate and highly-sexed; there was never a night when he wouldn't have sex when he was with her.

Emma was stunning, tall and blonde, with legs that reached her chin, but she was insecure, girly and clingy at times.

He went to the phone.

"Hi darling, it's Brendan. I'm off the rig tomorrow, getting the noon flight from Manchester so should be in about

4pm. Remember I have that course in Aberdeen next weekend so I'll be away for your birthday, but we can celebrate when I'm home."

"No problem Brendan, we're looking forward to seeing you," answered Carona.

They chatted for a while then said their goodbyes.

He went to the smoke room for a fag and then went back to the phone booth. It was the answering machine. *Lazy cow cannot be bothered crossing the room to answer the phone.*

"Hi Emma, its Brendan. Just to remind you I leave here tomorrow but I'm away on a course. I'll give you a call when I get there."

He put his head against the wall.

"Jeez, I need to start writing this down. I'll forget what I've said."

Nancy passed him in the corridor. He hardly recognised her – she looked stunning out of the kitchen, her red hair falling almost to her buttocks. She was wearing her tight lycra leggings and a figure-hugging T-shirt.

"You scrub up well girl, I never recognised you. Never knew you had that much hair under that hat of yours."

"Well, I'm full of surprises Brendan." She flashed a cheeky smile at him.

"Gotta go to the gym, it's really quiet down there at this time and I love having the place to myself," she said. She gave him a cheeky wink as she went up the stairs.

He watched as she climbed the stairs and he liked what he saw.

Brendan went to his cabin and changed into his gym gear. He was fit and toned with a good tan from his regular visits to Spain. He kept his tight curly hair short.

Nancy smiled as he came into the gym. He watched her as she sat on the floor in front of him; she had her legs out in front of her, putting her head to her knees as she stretched. He tried not to stare at her 'camel toe'. He had to concentrate hard to stop his erection.

"Good for you big boy, not seen you down here in ages," she said.

"Just too busy – never enough time," he smiled.

He positioned himself on the running machine, watching her in the mirror. He had never had a redhead; maybe this would be his first.

After a while, he came off the machine and rested. She was standing chatting to him, leaning on the arm of the bench press.

Fuck it, he thought, *worth a try – a hole's a hole.*

He moved closer to her and into her space. She smiled. He put his arm around her waist and kissed her. She responded. He lifted her up and put her on the bench.

She went straight for his member.

"You don't waste any time do you?" he smiled as he slipped his hand under her T-shirt, the sweat allowing his hand to slide easily over her abdomen. There was no fight, she wanted him. She moved her legs apart and lifted her bottom so he could take down her shorts.

He positioned her on the bench press and she laughed as he placed her legs in the arm press. He stared at her for a moment.

"You don't shave then?" he joked as he played with the golden triangle.

She enjoyed the roughness of his hands, the hard skin and calluses turned her on. He went over to the gym door, hung the 'cleaning' sign outside on the handle, and then put the lock on.

She was still in the same position when he came back, her pants on the floor and her white T-shirt pulled up around her breasts. He took no time in ploughing into her, her head hanging over the edge of the press. He caught their image in the mirror, her milk bottle skin just visible under his dark brown heavy frame. He had to cover her mouth to stop her screaming.

They sat for a while on the bench press, her head in his lap. Brendan unlocked the door and took the sign down.

Within minutes, the camp boss Malcolm came bumbling into the room.

"For fuck's sake, it's normally quiet in here. Prefer having the place to myself."

"Piss off then you fat twat and come back later," responded Nancy.

She was on the rowing machine, Brendan was running.

Malcolm sat on the bench press.

"Ugh, it's all sweaty and wet. Can people not use the bloody wipes to clean up after they use it?" He took a wipe from the box on the wall.

Brendan flashed a cheeky wink at Nancy who was already laughing so much she had lost her stroke.

So Your Wife Is A Man Then?

"Got some new porn when I was home," announced Ugly at the dinner table. "Do you want to borrow it Morgan to help you sleep?" he laughed.

"Yeah sure Ugly, I'll have a look. I like a good bit of porn," replied Morgan.

He was always curious to see what they were watching on the rig so he never declined an offer.

"It's these dirty bitches who shag other people's husbands, *Go Shag My Wife* it's called," said Ugly.

Maryanne was at the other table alone.

"Can you keep your voices down? It's disgusting talking about things like that. Men cheat on their wives too you know."

Ugly replied in his broad Glasgow accent, "Naw, ma wife knows better, she's lucky to have me. She knows I'd pure batter her if she shared her fanny with anybody else."

Ugly felt the usual pain in his abdomen as he made fun of his wife. He needed to stop these comments.

Maryanne ignored the comment.

"Well spunk bucket, what you got to say?" asked Ugly, looking sideways at Maryanne for a reply.

Maryanne stood up. As she passed him, she emptied the last of her juice over his head.

"Aw, that's love," laughed Ugly, "you so want me hen." He guffawed.

She left the room and ignored the laughter and clapping.

Terry was in his cabin. Her tired of the banter at times in the galley. Maryanne had ranted for ten minutes about Ugly,s comments. He had barely taken much notice of her; she took the hint and left him alone.

Terry knew of Katrina's death. Her dad had emailed him to tell him the news and that they were legally adopting Joshua. They knew Terry had been an important part of Alec's life. He also wanted to talk about Joshua's finances. Terry had to agree that it would be much more sensible for him to hand over any legal aspects that Alec had given him to the grandparents, and for them to choose who would take over if they where to pass away.

Terry knew Alec had been worried about Katrina getting her hands on the money; she would have wanted every penny.

It had been almost a year since the airport drama and the ridiculous proposal. Terry did love Stephen but he still had some issues about gay marriage. He had no idea why but he did, unlike Stephen who was ready to go with his silver top hat and white diamante-studded suit hanging in the wardrobe.

He still had a picture of Alec on his desk; he would talk to him sometimes, just like he did when he was alive. He still felt the pain of loss. He picked up the picture.

"Well buddy, there you go, old Patrick coming out of Narnia now. Here was us just thinking he liked his own company but he tells me he likes the girls *and* the boys."

He moved his fingers across the glass of the picture, kissed his fingers and placed them on Alec's photo. "Later buddy," he said, putting the picture back on the desk.

He wanted to show commitment to Stephen, he really did.

He lay on his bunk.

"Come on Alec, give me some advice. You were always good at that, help me out here, what should I do?" he glanced at Alec's picture, turned off the light and fell asleep.

He woke in a good mood, he felt upbeat. Not the normal feeling when offshore.

He turned the shower off. Then it came to him as he was shaving.

Fuck it, I'll ask Stephen to marry me. We can have whatever he wants; we're a long time dead. He felt a shiver down his spine and he laughed out loud at the sight of his foam-covered face in the mirror.

He hesitated as he went to close the cabin door; he popped his head back and looked at the picture of Alec.

"Thanks mate, you'd better be there!"

Terry decided that Patrick would be the best man; a substitute for Alec but he knew he would enjoy the campness that Stephen would inevitably organise.

Maryanne would be invited. They were good mates but he had no idea what she would think when he explained that Stephanie was Stephen. He would do that next week in the hotel when the crew changed. That was it for invites from the rig.

It was early December. The hotel was busy. There was a Christmas party going on in the room next to the bar. The atmosphere was good.

Terry decided he would speak to Patrick. Maryanne could wait.

He was surprised to see Maryanne on her own. He walked over to the bar.

"Losing your touch girl? Here on your own?" he asked. She swung around on the bar stool to face him.

"Nope Terry, believe it or not, I'm being good. I sort of bumped into an old colleague when I was home and he asked me out. As much as I love sex and it's hard to break my habit, I never shag around in a relationship. Never."

He gave her a hug and kissed her on the cheek.

"Well, you have the most brilliant time at home and I'll have some news for you next hitch, but I can't say any more at the moment."

She looked at the twinkle in his eye.

"Crikey Terry, look at you. Have you won the lottery?" She giggled.

Terry burst out laughing.

"Well, maybe I have," he said, putting his finger to his mouth and staring at the ceiling. "Or maybe, like you, I've realised people are more important than anything else."

She kissed him on the cheek.

"Right, I have to go to bed before I shag someone in here. I'm like a dog with a bone with testosterone," she sighed. He laughed out loud at her way with words.

Patrick had just come into the bar. He waved at Terry, winding his way through the crowd towards him.

"Patrick my man, I need to talk to you. Nothing to do with work," said Terry smiling. They found a quiet table at the far end of the bar.

"Loving the shirt Patrick. Everyone always looks so much better off the rig in their own clothes, don't you agree?"

"Yes, I agree Terry, but cut the pish. I'm intrigued by what you've got to tell me. You're not leaving the rig are you?"

"No, nothing like that."

Patrick edged forward and waited.

Terry leaned back in the green leather high-backed chair.

"Patrick, like I said at the time, I was honoured that you shared your sexuality with me and, no, I'm not going to ask for a shag." Both men burst out laughing at the same time.

"There is something I want to tell you about my life; Alec was the only person at work who knew."

Patrick was sitting with his chin resting on his joined hands, his elbows on the table.

"Stephanie, my partner in Tenerife, is actually Stephen. I've been gay since I was 18 and this year I'll have been with Stephen for all of 19 years. I hated lying to you as you are one of my dearest friends, if not *the* dearest. Close your mouth Patrick, I can see your tonsils!" said Terry.

Patrick shook his head and looked again at Terry.

"Are you taking the piss?" asked Patrick.

"No," replied Terry. He took his wallet out of his back pocket and showed him some pictures. Patrick broke into a smile as he looked at the photos.

"Well, who's a dark horse then?" said Patrick.

"Christ, I need another drink Patrick. Lager is it? I'm going for wine; I need a 'firkin' bucket of it. I've got even more to tell you, now you haven't run out the door," chuckled Terry.

Patrick sat and tried to take in what his big rugged pal had just told him. The more he thought about it, the more he laughed.

Terry came back with the drinks.

"Well Patrick, your thoughts then?"

Patrick sipped his drink, sat back in his seat and threw his arms in the air.

"Well, you fooled me. Never in my auntie's panties did I ever think you were gay. I feel privileged that you shared it with me, really I do." He clinked his glass against Terry's.

"Okay, are you ready for more?" asked Terry.

"Christ, are you wearing women's knickers under those jeans?" Both men roared with laughter.

"No Patrick, no!" He fell back in his chair and howled from his belly. "You see, Stephen wants to get married and I think it's all a bit 'poofy', this same-sex marriage thing. So I keep saying 'fuck off' every time he mentions it. However, I've decided I'm going to ask him this time home. He'll be so excited he'll be swinging from the lights. He has some sort of 'boggin' blingy wedding thing in mind. Anyways Patrick, to keep me sane throughout the big day, I want you to be my best man. You might even get picked up by one of Stephen's pals, there's plenty to choose from," he laughed.

He watched Patrick closely for his reaction.

Patrick felt the tears well in his eyes.

"Jesus Patrick, I didn't mean to upset you," said Terry.

"Come here ya dafty," said Patrick. He got up and went around the table to Terry. "Giz a hug big guy," insisted Patrick. Terry did as he was asked.

Patrick sat down and wiped his nose on one of the napkins on the table.

"Terry, I would be honoured, really I would."

"We're not wearing sequenced suits. Okay? Agreed?" said Terry, raising his glass.

"Agreed," laughed Patrick as they clinked their glasses in celebration.

They drank and laughed until they were thrown out at closing time.

Patrick was surprised he was inviting Maryanne but he didn't know what Terry knew about Maryanne's real life.

Maryanne had told Terry months ago about her difficulties at home. He was one of the few friends she had.

Patrick was easily sworn to secrecy.

A Hale Is A Hale...

Steve sat by the window in his flat in London. He was home for Christmas. He would rather have been working. He often thought of the family of the man that had died – he still felt guilty. He looked out across the London skyline from his top-floor vantage point.

He remembered the great Christmases he'd had when growing up in Edinburgh. He wondered if they all still got together on Christmas Eve. Did his mother ever think of him?

No one knew where he was now; he had lost touch several years ago. He thought it best that way. They would know he was out of prison. He would wait to see if they contacted him; he knew it was unlikely. They would have moved on with their lives.

The streets below were busy.

He jumped when his phone rang.

"Steve, is that you? It's Nancy from work. Is that you?"

"Yes Nancy, its Steve. What are you doing calling me on Christmas Eve?"

"Steve, I'm in a hotel in London, my bloody flight to Paris was cancelled. I'm supposed to be joining my brother and his family there for Christmas but now I'm stuck here. I just thought I'd see what you were doing."

He lay on the sofa looking at the ceiling.

"Well Nancy, I'm home alone and bored out my tits. Looks like we'd better do drinks and dinner."

"Brilliant Steve lad. How about 8pm, here at the hotel? I'll book a table." She gave him the details and hung up.

Steve jumped up and punched the air.

"Whoohoo, a night out!" he shouted. He went to get ready.

Nancy stood in her hotel room looking out across London. She could see Big Ben in the distance.

"Thank God I'm not on my own tonight," she said to her reflection in the window as she poured a glass of wine from the bottle sitting in an ice bucket.

She was always pleasing everyone else especially family and friends. Just because she was single, people felt sorry for her. Inviting her here and there, taking offence when she declined their offer. So most times she accepted, just to keep them happy.

She looked at herself in the mirror. *To be honest, I'll probably have more fun with Steve than I would in Paris.* The thought made her smile.

Nancy never 'got' the Christmas thing. She had grown up in Glasgow in a loving home with her parents and brother. She always puzzled why people would travel thousands of miles for one day; it was only a day. You can have a special day any time. She would have been happy being alone in her flat in Glasgow, no problem at all. But since her parents had died a few years ago, her brother insisted that if she was off the rig she should come to them. She made polite excuses, and one year even lied saying she was at work.

She loved wearing red but thought it made her look like a whore as it clashed with her red hair. She had her black velvet dress with her.

It was Christmas Eve. She wanted to feel special. She studied her reflection in the mirror. She knew she looked good. The dress clung to her small but perfect figure stopping halfway up her thighs and the cut showed her cleavage well.

Her hair was thick and curly after her shower, reaching her waist.

She slipped her feet into her black stilettos, giving her a little extra height. The little beaded black clutch bag and a simple gold chain around her neck completed the look.

Steve texted to say he was in the bar downstairs. She finished her wine and left.

Steve cut a smart figure. He was 5ft 8in with tight black curls kept short. He had gone for smart but not too formal. He had a pair of black dress trousers on, a sued dark brown waistcoat and a crisp white tuxedo shirt, but no tie. He left the top two buttons open, showing an adequate amount of chest hair but not too much. He had turned a few heads when he'd gone into the bar, he knew that. He sat at the bar and waited for Nancy.

He was reading the cocktail list. He noticed the barman look up from cleaning the glasses and several other people seemed to eye the door. Steve turned for a brief glimpse of what they were staring at: he had to take a second look. It was Nancy. He went towards her as she waited at the door. The light from the chandelier in the hotel lobby made her stunning hair look even better. *Pretty Woman* came to mind.

"Hey. Bloody hell, you're stunning. Look at you," he said.

"Oh, this old thing," she said laughing. He gave her a kiss on the cheek and went to the bar.

He wanted to stand up on the stool and shout, "Get it up ye, she's with me, haha!"

But he didn't.

"You look good Steve. I've never seen you out of jeans before."

"Aw, you know how it is, work and all. I'm really glad you called – made my night *and* my Christmas." They both laughed.

Nancy knew then that she would shag him. She was pleased she wouldn't be on her own tonight.

Steve was in his caveman mode. He was going to catch this piece of prey and little did he know she was already in his cave and ready to light his fire.

The Beautiful Ugly.

No one knew how Ugly had come by his name. He had a few front teeth missing. He could be inelegant and almost ignorant, but even Maryanne had admitted that he was not all 'ugly'.

He sat on the train. It was snowing outside. He was glad Christmas was over and New Year had begun.

He had lived in Glasgow all his life, born on 2 January 1963, Peter Joseph Giles. He grew up an only child, happy and loved. He adored the city and the memories it held of his forty-nine years on the planet.

The hospice was on the other side of the city. He had visited every day for the last year. When he was offshore, he would ring twice a day.

The heat was welcome on his face when he went into the hospice foyer. Ugly waved at the familiar faces of the staff on reception. The patients changed regularly, not unusual for *this* hospital ward.

People came here to die.

His wife had been moved from the hospital long-term ward next door to the hospice. He often drifted back to the 1980s when he had first met her, a blonde-haired Geordie lass, happy and carefree. Their life was good. He had always worked offshore and Janice married into the offshore life. She had no issues with her husband being away.

He remembered the phone call three years ago when he was at work. Alec was with him when he got the news.

Janice hadn't done anything different that day. She had put their 7-year-old twin girls Emily and Tabatha into the back of the car, and then headed for school as usual at 8.40am. The police said she probably never saw the lorry coming out from behind the parked bus. Its brakes had failed. The lorry smashed into Janice's car, pushing it across the road and crushing it again the wall of a house on the other side of the street. The children had died instantly.

Janice had been in a coma ever since. She had never woken up.

He looked at the shrivelled form in the bed, her skin like elastic over her bones, her aged face, and her moistened lips. He thought of the last time he'd seen his family the day he left. The children always cried when he went offshore, standing on the doorstep as he was driven off in a taxi. His wife would smile, knowing that in five minutes time they would be laughing and joking as she had planned a cake-making session. She had been brilliant at lifting their spirits.

Ugly stroked her hand and kissed her warm forehead.

She would be taken off her breathing machine tomorrow. It had been three years; there was now no hope. The decision had been made.

The guys would mock him at the hotel when the crew changed, calling him a big poof and a lightweight because he never drank. He had liked a drink before the tragedy but now he was scared that if he started to drink he would never stop.

No one on the rig knew his story. Alec was the only person who'd been on the rig with him at the time and now he was dead.

He was well-dressed in smart trousers, brogues and a long woollen coat. His black leather gloves gave him an air of sophistication. He'd been university-educated with a degree in economics. He'd gone to work offshore for a summer after graduation, he just never stopped. The money was alluring. Especially with twin babies!

He sat with Janice for a while. He spoke of Christmases past and of the excited girls and the fun they had on Christmas Day. He cried most days but the nurse told him that that was good.

He would be relieved when tomorrow was finally over; he had already grieved his wife's passing.

It was windy outside.

Ugly pulled his scarf tight and put his collar up. It was only 3pm but it was already getting dark. There were a few cars parked outside the graveyard but no one could be seen.

He opened the gate and followed the familiar path to his little girls.

Their headstone was in the shape of a little open book, their names and details in black on the white marble. He took the old flowers from the jar and put some new ones in that he'd bought at the hospice shop.

"Mummy will be with you soon my lovely girls. I hope you brush your teeth and comb your hair before she arrives." He kissed his hand and held it to the stone.

The wind was cruel; it swept up the snow and sent him looking for solace in the warmth of his scarf. The plot next to the children was already covered by a green tarpaulin in preparation for his wife's funeral later that week. It had all been arranged. He felt strange organising the funeral knowing which day Janice would die, but that was how she would have wanted it. Organised and with little fuss.

He held her hand as she slipped away.

The nurse who had cared for her on the long-term ward came in to say her goodbyes. Her son had been in the girls' class at school. She had looked after Janice all these years, before she had even been moved to the hospice.

He had left the room by choice when they removed her breathing tube. He heard the gasp from the corridor. She never fought, nor did she look in pain. She looked peacefully asleep.

Ugly buried his head in his wife's chest and sobbed. He imagined the girls at the end of the bed, taking a hand each and then going off together. As he sobbed, he wished he was with them too.

The staff were excellent. He was well-cared for in the following hours. A taxi was arranged to take him home. He sat by the phone in the evening and phoned those who needed to know.

He wanted this over with and to go back to work. To forget.

Offshore is a good place to forget.

He preferred being in his 'Ugly persona' than being Peter at these times in his life.

Marry me...

Stephen was waiting in the car.

It was too hot to walk to the terminal. He had the radio on and his seat reclined.

"Morning fella."

The voice made him jump, bumping his head on the roof of the car.

"For fuck's sake Terry, I nearly shit myself there."

Terry stood laughing as Stephen adjusted the seat and got out the car. Terry made a move to hug him. This shocked Stephen, he was puzzled, Terry never did this. It was always Stephen who had to make the first move in any tactile behaviour.

"Are you pissed?" asked Stephen.

"Oh, for goodness sake. Can I not give you a hug without having an intention or being intoxicated," moaned Terry.

He was taking the roof down. "I'll drive," he continued, "you enjoy the view and the air in your hair."

Stephen jumped into the passenger seat.

"Well, if you're not drunk, are you on drugs?" asked Stephen, smiling curiously at Terry.

Terry gave him a wide smile and a wink as he manoeuvred the car out of the car park.

"No, nothing like that you knob. Just happy to be home, and to see you."

"Anyway, have you got plans for tonight?" enquired Terry.

"No, nothing. You're usually tired and grumpy on your first night, so I haven't planned anything," Stephen replied.

"Good, good. I'm going to cook, so let's just pop to the supermarket. I can get everything now whilst I remember what I want to cook. I saw a nice recipe in the in-flight mag."

"Whoo hoo," laughed Stephen, "brilliant!"

Terry was sitting on the sun lounger by the pool. He watched Stephen swim. He was tall and well-tanned. He worked out and looked fit. His dark hair complemented his deep brown eyes.

He wondered why he was gay. He wanted to fancy women when he was younger, but they never gave him the same thrill as when he looked at men.

He listened to other people and their disgust at gay men and women, how it was 'not natural' and an illness. He had heard it all.

Gay people were no different to people in any heterosexual relationship, they just happened to be attracted to individuals of the same sex. Nothing else. In his opinion anyway.

He still got frustrated at holding back on conversations about his home life when at work. He wanted to boast about Stephen's singing career and his knack for cheering him up when he was down. All the things people speak about when talking about their loved ones.

Life was hard enough for everyone; it was unfair that the gay community had the extra burden of dealing with negativity. He agreed with some of their gay friends that it made them stronger people and there was a need to be very selective when choosing friends.

He threw Stephen a towel as he emerged from the pool.

"Okay. Kitchen's out of bounds until 7pm. You need to go out, I want the place to myself to get dinner ready," said Terry.

"I know, I know, you told me that already. I'm going up to work to practise a new routine, some new songs, and I'll be back by seven."

"If you're late, you'll get it boy, I mean it," laughed Terry.

Stephen waved through the patio doors as he left.

Terry stood back and looked at his masterpiece. The pool was the centrepiece of the patio. At the far corner, he had set up the table and, behind, the sun was setting over the ocean, with just some orange rooftops and a few trees in between. He laid a red tablecloth over a white one to give it a formal look. There was no wind. The white candle stood perfectly to attention as if it knew that it had an important role that evening.

He could hear the gentle lapping of the waves on the rocks in the distance, as if applauding his success this evening. The two champagne glasses had never been used; a present from Stephen's mum when they first moved in together.

Next to the table stood the wine cooler or champagne bucket as Stephen called it.

Terry felt emotional, the scene was perfect. He put some music on, a bit of 'Michael Ball', Stephen's favourite. It drifted across the patio, creating an ambience.

He heard the car pull up.

Terry stood leaning against the open patio door, a glass of wine in hand listening to Stephen's footsteps as he climbed the stairs that led from the carport to the patio.

Stephen stopped and stared. Terry smiled at the surprise on his face. Just for that moment in time, it had all been worth it. His face, that look.

"Evening Stevie boy," said Terry, raising his glass in the air and pouring another from the bottle on the little patio table. He picked up the glass and handed it to Stephen.

"Bloody fuckin' hell! What's all this for?" said Stephen. "Are you dying or something?" he asked.

Terry burst out laughing.

"No!" He pulled out a seat and beckoned Stephen to sit down.

"This is perfect. What a perfect night," he whispered to the dog that was now by his feet.

Terry was in the kitchen. He had a secret swig of chin. He was nervous.

He came back onto the patio and put a fresh bottle of champagne in the bucket next to the table.

Stephen lifted the bottle to look at the label. He nearly dropping it onto the floor when he saw Terry go down on one knee and take a ring from his top pocket.

"What the…"

"Stephen Evans, will you marry me?" He held out a white gold band with a small diamond in it, not masculine enough for Terry but he knew Stephen would like it.

"Are you taking the piss?" asked Stephen as he reached out for the ring. He knew by the look on Terry's face that he was serious.

He jumped from the table, tripping over the excited dog at his feet.

"Of course I will, yes."As he leapt into the air they both lost their balance, falling backwards into the pool. The little candle flickered at the breeze the men made, as if bowing in congratulations.

As they clambered out of the pool laughing, the sun bade its farewell on the horizon.

After they had changed and the food had been eaten, Terry told Stephen that they were going out at 10'clock so he should get changed again if need be.

"Oh, and by the way Stephen, you can have the biggest campest wedding you like. It's all over to you for planning." Stephen laughed, punching the air as he went inside to change.

"Where are we going Terry?" asked Stephen as they sat in the back of a cab.

"You'll see. We're celebrating."

The taxi climbed up towards the mountains, pulling up at the place where Stephen worked.

"Oh great, really original, a night at this place, and it's dead on a Wednesday." He rolled his eyes at Terry as they got out of the car.

"I thought you'd want to give everyone the good news," said Terry.

"Well yes, but Wednesday's 'no-show night', most people have the day off. Never mind, we're here now."

Terry followed Stephen into the club.

As they went into the main bar, the lights went up and Cliff Richards's *Congratulations* bellowed from the speakers.

The place was full of Stephens's friends and colleagues and a few of the people Terry knew on the island.

"Bloody hell Terry, you're full of surprises," laughed Stephen.

Time To Tell

The drill crew were in the departure lounge.

Brendan Hastings was sending his last text messages before turning off his phone for the flight to the rig.

It was a full flight, eighteen passengers and two crew. Brendan was sitting next to Ugly.

"You're quiet Ugly, did you have a good time off?" asked Brendan.

Ugly shifted in his seat. He was looking ahead at the wall.

"No, not really, my wife died."

Brendan spun around to look at him.

"What the fuck, oh my God, you poor man, I am so sorry," he replied.

None of the other crew had heard the conversation. Ugly was relieved as he scanned the faces for responses. None had noticed, they had their earplugs in ready for travel.

"Man, you should have taken some time off," said Brendan.

"To do what? Sit and feel sorry for myself? Not my thing, I'd rather be working."

Brendan never had time to reply as they were called out to board the helicopter. It is near impossible to speak to anyone in the helicopter.

They'd hardly been up in air and the airport was only just out of sight when the pilot spoke.

"We have a technical problem and we're returning to base."

The passengers looked at each other for reassurance. It was hard to have a conversation due to the noise, but the atmosphere changed.

They were turning now, heading back. As the helicopter approached the heliport the passengers could see the fire engines on standby. Without warning, the engine stopped as they were coming into land.

The helicopter landed with a hard thud on the tarmac. There was panic as they alighted. Brendan caught his belt on his life jacket on the chair at the door. He tripped and fell as he left.

The pain in his ankle was overwhelming.

"Oh for God's sake!" he shouted. One of the other passengers turned and came back to help him away from the chopper.

There was an ambulance on scene. Several passengers had bruises, non serious, but the event caused media interest.

It was the following morning before Brendan was interviewed by the aviation authority, along with the other passengers.

His name, and those of the other passengers had appeared in the papers and on the news. He was the only passenger who had remained in Hospital.

His next of kin had been contacted, the one he'd input on the Vantage system. This was something he'd thought long and hard about and he'd decided that he'd better change it to his brother, but he'd not got around to doing it – it was always too hectic at check-in. He left it as it was, with his Spanish wife Carona as the first contact.

Brendan was asleep when he heard her voice.

"Hello darling. My God, I'm so glad you're safe."

Brendan opened his eyes to see Carona by his bed. Her deep brown eyes were wet, she had been crying, he could see that. His heart jumped a beat.

Bloody hell, what if Emma turns up? He thought. She would have seen the news as well but received no phone calls. *Fucking hell, shit.*

He sat up in bed and watched Corona's mouth open and shut. He wasn't listening. He was working out how the hell he would get out of this one.

"The company have put me up in a hotel. How nice of them," said Corona. "They even organised a cab for me to come and visit you whenever I want. I'll stay until you're able to travel. We'll go home together," she said proudly in her sultry Spanish twang.

She explained that the children were with her mother. They could Skype them once he was feeling better.

When Carona left, Brendan asked after the other passengers.

"Oh, they've all been discharged. Only you to fuss over now," smiled the nurse. "You're quite a celebrity Brendan. Apparently, one of your colleagues pulled you free from the damaged helicopter. Your friend was on GMT this morning and your picture seems to have been all over the media in the last twenty-four hours."

Brendan smiled, but said nothing.

Later that day, Brendan was in the toilet. He looked at his reflection, unshaven and tired. He looked pale.

He heard the voices outside.

"Oh okay, I'm a little confused. I thought Mrs Hastings had been in earlier this morning. I must have made a mistake," said the nurse.

He felt sick to his stomach. He wanted to run but he had nowhere to go except down the toilet pan. He was even stupid enough to look at the ceiling tiles in the toilet, wondering whether he could get out that way.

He opened the door and went back into his little single room. Emma was standing with her back to him looking out the window.

"Oh hi Emma, I was going to call you," he limped around the bed supporting himself on the wall. She helped him to ease himself and his plastered leg onto the bed.

She kissed him.

"I was so worried Brendan, no one called. I tried loads of times to call the number that came up on the TV but they wouldn't give me any information. They said I was not down as next of kin." She rearranged his pillows.

"I'm sorry Emma. I put my brother Alistair down, but he's on holiday in the States. I meant to tell you about that as I always worried that if this happened and the police turned up at the door, it'd be better for you to hear from my brother first."

"I've never met him Brendan so it would make no difference to me."

It was perilously dangerous.

Deep in his stomach Brendan was excited at the predicament, but in his head he was scared. He was in a corner, like a deer in the headlights.

After Emma had left, he sat looking out the window. He saw the reflection of the nurse behind him in the window. She was watching him from the door. He knew she knew, he could tell by her look.

Deep down, he could sense there was danger…

The nurse was doing her evening drugs round. She saw Emma walking up the corridor and not far behind her was another woman coming out of the lift.

The nurse locked her trolley. She could smell an imminent 'situation'. She had worked in Emergency for many years; she had learned to identify the 'scent' of danger before it erupted.

She went into Brendan's room.

"I think you might be in trouble," she said, standing with her arms folded at the door.

"What do you mean?" asked Brendan with a startled but pathetic look on his face.

"Well, the 'two' Mrs Hastings are coming up the corridor now. I think your game is up Brendan."

She went to the nurses' station and waited.

Emma went into the room and shut the door. Carona watched through the little porthole window as Emma kissed him and fussed over his pillows.

The nurse watched on as Carona opened the door.

She said nothing to the doctor or the nurse who were standing either side of her as she picked up the phone and called security, much to the bemusement of the other members of staff who had no idea what was going on.

Brendan was sitting on the bed. The nurse could only hear the sound of indistinct and raised voices. She saw the chair fly towards the bed, landing on Brendan.

The two women were fighting.

The security guard was trying to get into the room but the women were scrapping on the floor blocking the door. Brendan was off the bed and standing with his hands on his head, watching the women punching and kicking each other.

Brendan said nothing as he was escorted off the ward; he was looking down at the floor. The handcuffs were attached to the wheelchair.

The Secrets At The table.

Patrick the OIM put the phone down; he leaned back in his chair. *My God, you could not make this up.*

HR had called and told him of Brendan's fate.

He had been instantly dismissed due to the huge news coverage. The revelations of his two marriages being uncovered due to the crash had reached fever pitch in the media.

Patrick called a meeting with heads of department. He would give them the facts as per HR information before the story grew 'arms and legs' on the rig.

"Oh, it's better than *Corrie,*" laughed Maryanne. "I had no idea, no idea at all. Thirteen years. Oh my God!"

She stood up, walked to the mirror and pushed her hair behind her ears. "He was a bloody good shag anyway," She thought to herself, before going back to the group of men gathered around the oval table.

Everyone had an opinion.

It was a bit like the meeting of the cardinals to choose a new pope. They all appeared innocently surprised at Brendan's sordid secret.

Who was to know what lies beneath the surface of the people around the table? Thought Patrick as he scanned the people in the room. Even he had his secrets, big juicy ones!

There was Maryanne, the nympho, pretty and ladylike.

Steven the ex-con, clean-shaven, polished face, articulate and confident.

Patrick, who liked 'willie' more than 'fanny' but enjoyed both.

The camp boss Malcolm who was tutting and shaking his head. His breath still smelt of the three or four bottles of vodka he put away each day at home. A wife-beater.

Morgan was representing the maintenance department. His checked shirt and tidy little moustache gave him a 'protective shell alias' – 'Rancoon Ravatt' to millions of porn viewers.

Terry said nothing. He liked Brendan. He had his own secrets.

For The Love Of A Family.

Malcolm was glad to get home. It had been a busy trip.

"Hey bitch, come and say hello to your old man then," he shouted whilst looking up the stairs.

He threw his bag into the corner and went into the kitchen. He took a glass from the cabinet and opened the cupboard. It was empty.

His wife was called Mable.

She crept quietly into the room. She was a small grey-haired woman of Chinese origin, slightly built with olive skin. Her eyes were dark and lifeless. She looked like a mechanical human, her face appeared emotionless. She stood at the door, looking at the floor. She seemed to be waiting for something.

"Where is the drink you useless cow? Three weeks I've been away. What have you done apart from talk crap on the computer to your peasant family in China?" She looked up at this remark. "Oh yes, the dear family, dare I mention them?" he scorned, waving his hands mockingly at her.

Malcolm grabbed her by the hair and pulled her backwards. She never fought back, she was used to this.

"Where is my fucking drink? Get out of here and get me a drink now, or else you know what will happen."

Mable scurried to the door, took the car keys and left.

She never looked at anyone in the supermarket. She had lived in the town with Malcolm for nine years after he brought her over from China. Her family were so proud of her marriage to a British man.

She took the six bottles of vodka to the self-service checkout. She avoided people at all costs; she'd been warned by Malcolm that he would kill her and her family if he saw her talking to anyone.

She heard the music blaring out as she got out of the car. He was in the kitchen. She put the bottles on the table.

"Come and dance with your husband," demanded Malcolm, grabbing her by the shoulder and throwing her around the room.

He poured two glasses, offering one to her. She bowed and shook her head.

"You know I don't drink Malcolm," she whispered.

"Oh fuck off then." He threw the half-full glass in her face. She scurried out the room and up the stairs.

"Silly bitch! I should've left you prostituting in China where I found you," he shouted after her.

She heard him fall up the stairs. It was always the same.

He fell in the bedroom door, landing on his knees next to the bed.

She lay there as he tried to have sex with her, his huge belly pressing on her intestines. She knew he would fall asleep, he always did. She wriggled from under him and moved to the edge of the bed. She took out the little photo from the cabinet next to her bed and gave goodnight kisses to the images of her mother, father and sisters.

The tears came like an alarm clock. She slept.

She was in the garden when he awoke. She saw him in the kitchen.

"Coffee, now!" he shouted down the garden.

She left the greenhouse and made him a coffee. She thought of poisoning him sometimes but she didn't know how to do it. He sent her family money every month. They would starve without his generosity. That was the only reason she stayed.

They were in the car on the way to the supermarket. She was not allowed in the front seat.

"You smell of urine, so get in the back," he would say.

She would watch the world go by as they drove through town. When she was sore, she wanted to open the window and shout for help but she knew that he would probably kill her if she did. She watched the rain splash against the window; her reflection mirrored the rain like tears on her cheeks, they suited her mood perfectly.

It was always the same in the shop. Malcolm was a gentleman to neighbours or anyone that knew them. She was trained to behave. She smiled and nodded. "Her English is poor," he would say to people.

She spoke excellent English.

She had been to university but had had to leave before graduating as her father had lost his job. She had turned to prostitution to put food on her family's table. She had told her parents that she had a job in a 'call centre'. They believed her. She had been picked up by Malcolm one evening when he was on holiday.

A charming Englishman who offered to look after her.

She had married him quickly, but it was only two weeks before the abuse began.

Every day was the same. Would she be hit today, stood on, peed on, or raped?

She was unpacking the shopping when he started.

"I saw you talking to the guy on the bakery counter, you slag."

He held his drink next to his chest, his other hand leaning on the kitchen unit.

"No Malcolm, he spoke to me, I just nodded back. I didn't speak, I promise I didn't."

He lifted his hand and smacked her across the face with the back of his hand; her head shook but she remained on her feet. He grabbed her face and pushed her backwards onto the table in the middle of the room. She dropped the rice bag she was holding, it burst and scattered onto the floor like millions of little people running for cover under the kitchen units, hiding from the roaring dragon above them.

"Look at the mess you daft pheasant, clean it up now!" he pushed her onto her knees.

She knelt with her head down, her arms close to her ribs, in case he would kick her; she was prepared. She had been beaten many times over the years but she had only been to the hospital once with burns to her leg when he had set fire to her dress one evening. He had laughed as she ran to the kitchen sink to dowse the flames. She told the staff in A&E that she'd caught it on the coal fire. They didn't have a coal fire.

She stayed there on the kitchen floor until he left the room.

She cleaned up the mess and unpacked the rest of the shopping. Her face was throbbing but she was used to that.

He only slapped her twice more that day. She was relieved when he pushed her head down the toilet in the evening, as the cold water eased the pain from the slap marks on her face.

Even tigers can Cry...

The drill floor was slippy. The weather had been terrible.

"What a bloody miserable job this is," said Ugly to one of the new roustabouts.

This was Oliver's first time offshore; he had paid for his entire course himself, waiting two years for a break.

He was delighted when the company had offered him a three-month trial.

Ugly liked him. He was organised, keen and asked lots of questions.

"You need to get some thermals lad. Gets worse than this sometimes," said Ugly.

He watched as Oliver's hands shook with the cold whilst they tightened the bolt on the pipe they were fitting.

The wind and the rain were battering them head on.

"Come on lad; let's go get a coffee, warm us up a bit."

Oliver flashed him a smile and nodded in agreement.

The boot room was busy; the rain had limited what they could do outside on the rig.

Brendan had never reached the rig after his conversation in the departure lounge with Ugly. He was now in prison, a bigamist.

Ugly had taken a helicopter to the rig the day after the emergency landing episode. He was uninjured, so declined any time off to recover. He just wanted to get back to work.

No one knew of his wife's death.

Both men found a seat. Oliver was still shacking with the cold.

Ugly could see that he was grateful for some heat. The boy looked a lot younger than his 26 years. He had told Ugly of all his great plans to make the most of his new salary. This pleased Ugly as it reminded him of similar plans that he'd had many years ago. He thought maybe that was what he liked about him; he was a historical shadow of his own past.

Maryanne breezed into the room.

"Nothing to say for yourself then Ugly?" she asked as she went to the coffee machine. "I see you have a new wee boyfriend," she smirked as she nodded at Oliver.

The new lad smiled, not quite sure how to deal with this confrontation. He thought it best to watch and learn.

The boot room erupted in laughter at Maryanne's comment. She liked that. She had their attention.

A voice across the room shouted, "Bet your wife will be glad you've got wee Oliver to play with at work. She'll be glad of the peace when you get home 'cos you'll have used up all your sex drive at work."

Maryanne cackled and looked at Ugly for a reaction.

Ugly blew on the top of his drink, watching the steam rise up. He could mock his darling wife no more, it was time.

He looked up.

"Oh yes, she has peace. She died last week when I was at home," he announced. "There, I've said it. You all know now."

Toby put his arm on Ugly's shoulder.

Ugly sipped his coffee. He felt embarrassed.

The silence was deafening.

He went over to the counter and put this coffee on the table. "I need a smoke."

Maryanne followed him out the room.

"I'm sorry, I had no idea. Oh my God man, I am *so* sorry."

Ugly nodded at her comment and went into the smoke room shutting the door behind him. She stood in the corridor, placing her head against the wall, feeling stupid, embarrassed and angry that she had not noticed the change in his personality. She thought it was just the helicopter thing and the Brendan saga.

You stupid cow, she thought

When Strangers Know...

Mable was glad her husband's three weeks at home was almost up.

She knew she needed to change things but she had no friends or family nearby to help. She had convinced herself that he must not stop her family's money. She needed a purpose to live and providing for her family back in China was her escape from taking her own life.

She and her family were Malcolm's prisoners.

She knew things were better in China; things had moved on for her family since her arrival in the UK nine years ago.

Her father now had a job and her two sisters were also working. She was sure that if her parents knew how badly Malcolm was treating her, they would tell her to return home immediately. They could manage without his money.

He was leaving in an hour. He was at the door with his bag.

"The taxi's here, I'm going," he shouted.

He opened the front door that looked onto a little front garden and onto the house opposite. The taxi was behind the hedge at the roadside.

She came out of the kitchen, flicked the hall light on and walked towards him.

"Remember, you step out of line and your family starve."

He lifted his hand and held her chin between his finger and thumb, forcing her false teeth to protrude from her mouth. She'd had all her own teeth when she married him, however because of the beatings they had gradually fallen out over the years. She couldn't remember what she had told the dentist. She had made up so many stories over the years on visits to the GP, A&E and the dentist that she had lost track of them all.

The front door was open.

Mable went to move to let him pass but she tripped on his bag and fell over it. She put her hand out against the wall to stop the fall.

"My bag, you clumsy immigrant!" he growled.

He pushed her out of the way, leaving her in a heap on the floor. He then shoved her legs aside with his feet, making sure he stood hard on her ankle. Mable clambered up, her ankle throbbing. She spotted the face of her neighbour watching from her upstairs bedroom window but she had let the net fall back when Mable caught her eye.

She stood with her back against the closed door; she wondered if the woman across the road had seen what Malcolm had done to her.

She ran upstairs to email her family. He was gone.

She was free for three weeks.

Peeking 'Out The Closet...

The pub was quiet.

"I love this time of year. It's nice and peaceful. We can even have a conversation without shouting," said Maryanne as she sat down at the table next to Terry and Patrick.

"What's with the 'no-man rule' then?" asked Patrick, looking at Maryanne.

She flicked her hair back.

"Well, I'm seeing someone at home, an old colleague, so I'm saving myself." She smiled at the two men who were on the opposite side of the table.

"Yes, I'm gagging for it but I have morals." She laughed with the men as she listened to their hearty chuckles.

"I've a secret to tell you Maryanne," said Terry.

She sat forward, her pupils dilating. "Oh go on then, I'm waiting."

"I'm getting married."

She jumped over and hugged him with a whoop of glee. *Hope she rots in hell*, she thought but she bit her lip to stop herself from saying what was on her mind.

"Oh, I thought you and Stephanie were already married," she said, flashing a smile and sweeping her hair back over her shoulder.

"Champagne. I'll get some champagne." She jumped up and glided to the bar in her well-practised sultry walk. Terry rolled his eyes at Patrick, both men doubled-up with laughter.

She strutted back from the bar with the bottle in her hand and three 'flutes' in the other.

"Oh, you must be so excited," gushed Maryanne with her saliva almost dripping like a rabid dog. Patrick bit his lip to stop his laughter. She was so jealous even a two-year-old could have picked up the scent.

"You must come to the wedding," said Terry, "it would be fun."

"Oh, I would love to meet Stephanie. Any excuse for a hat, that's me." She placed the three glasses on the table.

Terry put his hand on her forearm.

"Maryanne, I need to tell you something, it's about Stephanie."

"Oh, she's not terminally ill or anything is she?" she asked, secretly hoping she was.

"No, she's not, because *she* is a *he*. My partner's name is Stephen."

Maryanne sat facing him. She blinked. Patrick was going blue as he tried to contain a giggle.

"I'm gay Maryanne, that's why you never got my willy."

She glanced quickly at both men.

"You're having a laugh, you bastards." She squealed with laughter.

She noticed Terry taking a photo from his wallet. She stared in disbelief at the picture of the two men.

"Oh my God! Oh my God!" she screeched so loud it attracted some looks from the bar staff and the few people who were in the bar.

"You're gay," she said again.

"For fuck's sake, keep your voice down you gob shite," growled Patrick.

"Jeez, you're a dark horse," she said, downing her glass in two gulps. She picked up the other glasses that the men had not touched and drank them down in one swoop.

She was smiling, but inside she hurt. Secretly, she was very fond of Terry but now he'd kicked her in the teeth. She knew now that she would never get him into bed. Of course, she would never stop trying; at least if her current relationship ended. That was just the way she was.

She filled up their glasses and joined in the conversation.

When A Stranger Changes Your Life...

It was about 4pm.

Mable was in the kitchen sitting at the table reading her latest book when the doorbell rang. She never had any visitors, she was not allowed friends, she didn't know any of her neighbours and the postie always came in the morning.

She put her book down and went to the door. She recognised the lady from the house across the road. They had only ever waved and nodded, they had never spoken. She was well-dressed, about the same age as Mable.

She had a book in her hand.

"I hope you don't mind me bothering you. I'm Sally Hughes from number 97 across the road." She waited to be invited in.

She could see the unease on Mable's face, and the bruises on her neck and arms. She had no time to apply the usual make up or foundation to cover them, she was caught 'off guard'.

"Please come in," beckoned Mable. "My husband is away offshore if it's him you've come to see," she said, looking at the floor as she spoke.

They made their way into the kitchen.

"Oh, I won't stay," said Sally. "I just came over to drop a book off. I know you visit the library nearly every day when you're on your own. I would do the same if I had the time," she laughed.

They made polite conversation before Sally went, leaving the book on the table. "I'll see myself out." Then she was gone.

Sally closed her front door leaning her back against it, her head pressed back. *Poor cow, he must hit her stupid,* she thought. She planned to help her, but not to interfere. *Bastard offshore worker. Beer-swigging, wife-battering sod.*

She would go back at the end of the week for the book and then try and have a conversation with her.

She had been married to an offshore worker years ago. She was sure they were all the same. She'd never been hit but he was never sober enough to have a conversation. This guy seemed worse. She thought all offshore men should come with warnings attached to them; not the women who worked offshore of course, they were brave and 'new age'.

Mable picked the book up to look at the cover.

I can see the sky read the title.

The blurb told of a girl's imprisonment in a house in London, battered by her husband and used as a sex slave. Not quite her circumstance.

Or was it?

She fished her chores and went back into the kitchen. She fingered the cover of the book for a few minutes before picking it up. She read the blurb again. She made a coffee.

With the book and beverage in hand, she went into the garden. She thumbed the pages and began to read.

Mable felt a long-gone fire in her belly. She blushed at the feeling, it felt wrong. If *he* could see her now he would hit her.

She thought the light had gone out, kicked out of her by *him*. But it was still there, it just needed fuel.

She cried and laughed out loud as she read the book. She was reading her autobiography. This was *her* last nine years laid out in print in front of her.

The moon was high in the sky when she closed the book. She had not noticed the cold night air.

She was angry. She had not felt angry for a long time.

She was thinking so fast she felt dizzy.

She felt as if the Mable she knew had come back from the dead, or had *escaped* from captivation. She held the book close to her chest like a maiden clutching her knight in shining armour before he went into battle.

She smiled to herself as she skipped up the garden and into the house.

It's All Going On Offshore..

"Oh for Christ's sake," shouted Morgan the mechanic across the rig tannoy system. "Will whoever keeps putting their 'fanny pads' down the toilet stop it now?"

The Patrick the OIM put his hands on his head as the tannoy announcement cut off.

"Oh gimme strength," he grated under his teeth. He prepared for an onslaught of complaints about Morgan's announcement.

Down in the septic tank, Morgan sat deflated. He had been cleaning out a blocked pipe, his eyes level with the opening, when, without warning, a used sanitary towel flew out of the pipe with full force and hit him in the face, clearing the obstruction, but showering him with the remnants that had been stuck behind the offending item.

"Look at me," he cursed under his breath, taking in the murky and smelly deposits in his hair and on his overalls. He heard the tones he expected on the radio.

"Get up here now you." Screamed Patrick the OIM.

He replied, "Yes, yes, on my way and ready for a battering."

He climbed from the septic tank, cleaned himself up and went off to meet the 'firing squad'. He felt like a lost soldier going over the top from his bunker during the Great War.

He was thankful that he stank so much it forced Patrick to be swift in his dressing-down as he couldn't stand the smell; Morgan smirked as he left the office.

Nancy was feeling sick. She had been vomiting non-stop for a week now. She was waiting for Maryanne to come on board. she was too embarrassed to see Paul, the male medic. He was hugely handsome and she didn't trust herself in his company in a locked sickbay; she would have dropped her pants for him in a second.

She had smoked a bit of dope on her last trip home. She thought maybe that was it. Her periods were normal so she didn't fear the worst.

As she stood at the server in the galley she felt dizzy. She held onto the side of the bain-marie server unable to control the projectile vomit that flew over the food and onto those waiting to be served on the other side of the hatch. She felt her knees give way beneath her. Fortunately, two of the galley stewards grabbed her and helped her to a seat at the back of the galley.

Malcolm stormed in from the back store.

"You stupid whore! You've ruined the food; you deserve a kicking for that." He lifted his right foot ready to kick her directly in the head, but was rugby-tackled by one of the stewards, sending him across the kitchen floor. He landed in a heap by the sink. He sat there for a while on a warning not to move as the medic helped Nancy out of the kitchen and into the sickbay.

"You're a twat," said Patrick as they sat in his office. "Why would you want to kick her when she's ill? You need help man, that violent streak will get the better of you one day."

Malcolm left the office. He was angry that he'd let his guard down. If that had been his wife, he would probably have kicked her to death.

Nancy was resting in the sickbay.

She lay on the couch looking up at the lights on the ceiling. The injection that Paul the medic had administered had helped. She was too exhausted to fancy him; she was just grateful for his care.

"Right Nancy, I need to do a few tests and I need a urine sample. If you're okay with it, I'll need to do a pregnancy test. It's just a process of elimination to try and find out why you have been vomiting, nothing else. It's all confidential," he assured her.

Paul had seen it many times before, pregnancy was not uncommon offshore.

Nancy had been in the sickbay almost two hours. The medic was sitting next to her when she woke up..

"Just a nasty urine infection, we will get you home, tomorrow once you are rested." Said the medic.

She was relieved she was not pregnant. She and Steven had spent three days in the hotel room naked for most of the time. Only dressing when room service arrived with fodder and drinks

Give me A Tsunami Any day

"This is not a drill! This is not a drill!" wailed an authoritative Patrick across the tannoy. It was 11pm.

"Go to your allocated muster stations and check in with your muster checkers."

The rig was full.

Maryanne was always frustrated by the assortment of gear people brought to a muster. She explained what to bring during the induction to the rig, but still people trundled to the muster with the wrong kit. One girl even had her handbag over her shoulder. *Inductions were important but a thankless task*, she thought.

Ugly was sitting in the TV room, he had only been in bed an hour. Next to him sat a third party employee, a girl from overseas. He glanced at her sitting with her life jacket on her knee, dressed in a pair of shorts and a vest.

"Where the fuck are you planning to go dressed like that, Tena fuckin' reef? It's an oil rig in the middle of the North Sea; you'll not last five minutes in the lifeboat dressed like that."

She stared in horror at Ugly.

"Oh, you bad, bad man. That's not a nice thing to say to me. I have a degree you know. I'm scared now," she replied.

"Yeah, be fuckin' scared hen. You'll be stiff and dead in no time if we go outside. A degree in how to be a bloody thick cow, I'd say." There were pockets of laughter.

Patrick was waiting anxiously for a radio report. Smoke had been detected in the engine room.

It seemed to be forever before the muster count met the correct number. Patrick was fuming when the barge engineer called on the radio, "We only have eighty-nine people, should be ninety." The cabin search took fifteen minutes.

"Jeez, if this was abandonment, we'd be fucked," shouted the OIM, making sure the radio and tannoy were at the off button. No one in the radio room commented. They knew when to stay quiet.

"Found him," came a voice on the radio. "It's Todd Evans, he was asleep in 304," said the barge engineer over the radio.

"That bloody boy," screeched the OIM, "might be the most academic roustabout we've ever had but he's as thick as bloody porridge. These academics do my friggin' head in." He banged his fist on the desk table.

No one made eye contact with an angry OIM during a muster.

The drill came to an end and everyone returned to a normal evening offshore.

It had been two weeks since Sally had dropped the book off at her 'battered' neighbour. She was in the front garden cutting the grass. In the corner of her eye, she saw a taxi pull up. It was empty. She was sure he had another week to go offshore.

She watched as Mable emerged from the front door. One case, two cases and then three. Her heart missed a beat. She walked to the front gate. Mable gave the cases to the driver.

She crossed the road to where Sally was standing and handed the book back to her.

"Thank you for this. It was just what I needed." The women stared at each other for a few seconds as if understanding exactly what each other were thinking.

"I'm going home now, back to my family in China. Reading that book made me realise what is important and what is wrong. Thanks to you, I will have a future without misery." She squeezed Sally's arm, turned and left.

She looked at the taxi driver, took a deep breath, and began some idle chat about the weather. She had begun her *escape*.

Hours later, Sally saw another taxi pull up.

She watched from behind her bedroom curtains as he stood looking up at the dark windows of the house. Her heart raced with excitement as he closed the door behind him. The lights went on, one after another.

She watched Malcolm scurry from room to room and back again. There was a stream of water running from the front door. She saw him searching the wardrobes and the cupboards. The curtains were wide open.

She thought it was better than having the best seats at the cinema. She smiled as she closed her blinds.

Mable sat back in her first class seat, a present she had given herself on Malcolm's credit card. She had emptied the bank account, the details of which she had carefully noted over the years, saving the information from his internet banking site when he left it open in his drunken states.

She had deleted all her family contacts. She had never told him that her family had moved to another part of China because of her father's new job.

She thanked the cabin crew for the cocktail. She sat back and waved goodbye to the UK out the window. She sipped the drink slowly, smiling to herself as she remembered turning the heating on full and leaving the plug in the bath. Oh, and she had 'forgotten' to turn the tap off.

The four sofas, three fridges, six cookers and five top-of-the-range beds would arrive tomorrow. She giggled as she savoured the cocktail.

She felt satisfied with her revenge.

Just Call Me Janice He Said....

The wedding had been a great day. Patrick and Terry had travelled back that morning from Tenerife.

They were exhausted.

Patrick looked at the email for the third time. He was very open-minded, even more so since his 'educational trip' to the wedding, and a week with Stephen's 'friends'.

He had a 'sore bum', but he'd had a great time.

Is someone taking the bloody piss? He thought.

Terry wandered in with a cup of coffee for him, putting it on the desk and plonking himself in the seat next to Patrick.

"Anything interesting then?" he asked Patrick.

Patrick was uneasy in his seat.

"What? Share then," said Terry.

Patrick scratched his head and rubbed his chin.

"We have a new barge engineer coming next week – Paul Jones – have you met him?" asked Patrick.

"Not a name I know of. Should I?" asked Terry, peering at the troubled expression on Patrick's face.

"Well, his name is Paul but we have to call him 'Janice' when he gets here."

Terry screwed up his face.

"What the fuck is that about?" he laughed.

Patrick looked again at the e mail.

"He is living as a woman so he can have a sex change in the future. Apparently, that is part of the process." Both men burst out laughing.

The anticipation of meeting 'Janice' soon grew. Only Patrick, Terry and the medic knew of the gentleman's situation. It would be up to *him* to manage the rest.

Maryanne had arrived the previous day. She loved this sort of thing. "Oh I love individuals" was her response.

Patrick was at his desk when he came in to introduce himself.

"Hello, I'm Janice James, the new 'bargie'."

Patrick had prepared his professional face but he was not prepared for this.

Stood in front of him was a six-foot tall bloke built like a rugby player with three days of growth on his face, the deepest Welsh accent and not a feminine bone in his body.

Patrick stood up and shook his hand.

"Janice eh? Well, you're in for a roller coaster of a trip lad." He smiled and waited for a response.

Janice laughed, flashing his immaculate white teeth at him. Patrick felt himself blush.

He'd get it, thought Patrick, trying to maintain his decorum. He was sure he noticed the guy pick up on his little 'bisexual' radar.

They never expected the helicopter.

It was Arthur, a very quiet and unassuming radio operator – in fact a boringly boring radio operator – who had called the OIM to say they had a helicopter arriving in an hour.

After a swift call to the office, it was confirmed that medical staff were coming to do an on-the-spot drugs check. Patrick sensed the atmosphere change on the rig as soon as he had made the announcement. He knew some crew would be caught out. It only ever happened rarely but when it did he always lost someone.

There was the usual row of men at the end of the day sitting outside the sickbay, unable to pee in front of another person; the ones who admitted that they sat down in public toilets to pee and never understood why women got cubicles but men had to use a trough. Women went to the toilet together, why should they not have to perch on troughs? They could still chat as they peed and do their make-up at the same time.

Only six crew had tested positive for some sort of substance.

One of the nurses who had travelled with the team seemed disappointed in their catch as she presented the names to the OIM. Patrick could only wonder why such an individual who works in the so-called caring profession of nursing could be so taunting and victorious at the thought of these six people's lives being ruined.

He stared in disbelief at the disappointment in her expression as she discussed their findings.

"Oh well, we've only got six out of ninety today," said the nurse in a droned Aberdonian accent.

"Six too many for me love. Poor guys will lose everything now, job, family and friends. A bit of fucking sympathy would not go amiss you hard-nosed cow," replied Patrick.

The nurse said nothing and didn't even raise an eyebrow.

"Fat-arsed bitch," he hissed under his breath as she left.

In contrast, the doctor and another nurse who came to see him before they left were as professional as he would expect if he was being treated in hospital.

"Pity how one bad egg can let your team down," he said to them as they left. The 'bad egg' was hovering at the door.

The nurse and doctor exchanged glances but remained silent.

Patrick spoke to the six individuals before they left, giving them a copy of the company's 'misuse of drugs' policy.

He shook their hands as they departed for the helicopter. He was angry with them, but he also had sympathy.

Maryanne and Steven stood silently beside him. He wished the visiting medical team well, shaking their hands. But he ignored the pompous nurse as she left, leaving her looking flustered and awkward.

He watched as the helicopter flew off. He went to the office and called HR to organise replacements.

He hated days like this offshore.

Surprise Surprise...

Ugly sat watching TV at home.

It was a beautiful summer's evening.

crime stopper was coming on. He glanced at the TV occasionally as he thumbed the evening paper. Some story about paedophilia and wanted men.

Something caught his eye.

He put the paper down and turned the volume up. He used the rewind button on his remote. He went closer to the TV.

It was him, or his double. It was Arthur, the radio operator from the rig.

He called Terry at home.

"Can you get the same programmes over there, as here?" he asked.

"Yeah, we can. Why?"

He explained what he had just seen.

"Mother Jesus. It's him. Bloody hell," said a shocked Terry. They talked for a while then ended the call.

Ugly rang the number on the screen.

He soon got a call back. He told them what he thought. He didn't feel guilty. If it was a mistake then so be it. These people were monsters.

Arthur Fleming had been a radio operator offshore for many years. He never stayed anywhere more than three years. He moved house regularly too. "A rolling stone and all that," he would say when asked about his next move.

He had few friends on the rig, keeping himself entertained with his matchstick models and reading.

Patrick heard the chopper.

"It's bloody nearly midnight, what's going on?" Jessica, the night radio operator, was in a fluster. She knew nothing of the helicopter until ten minutes before it landed. She was frantically trying to get the heli Deck crew in place.

"It's a police helicopter," she squealed as Patrick stormed into the radio room.

"They won't tell me anything on the radio. What should I do?"

"Let them land," said Patrick.

He changed his shirt, brushed his teeth and went up to meet the arrivals.

The two police officers introduced themselves to the OIM and went to his office.

Patrick sat with his mouth wide open

. He showed the men to *the* cabin.

Patrick stood in heli Admin, the blinds flicked open in the radio room which looked onto where he was standing. Lots of pairs of eyes with dilated pupils watched as Arthur the radio operator was led to the helicopter in handcuffs.

Arthur didn't look anyone in the eye. He stared straight ahead.

Patrick was relieved it had been straightforward. Had the crew known his crime, God knows whether he would have made it to the helicopter alive.

Patrick never prayed, but as he lay in bed he said, "Please God, no more. An abandonment, a tidal wave or a tsunami would be fine, but no more of this."

Malcolm was in the radio room. He fancied Jessica the radio operator. She was in her 50s and a bit timid, just the type he could manipulate.

Jessica was too polite to be rude.

"We should have a night out Jessica, when we get to the beach," said Malcolm, wiping the saliva from his mouth on his sleeve. He moved and sat in front of the microphone, his knees just touching her forearm on the desk.

"Oh, I'm really busy Malcolm. I have my horse and all to look after," she replied, flicking her hair but avoiding his gaze.

"Come on Jessica, it would be fun," he urged, placing his finger on the back of her hand and running his nail up her arm.

"Please don't do that." She brushed his arm off, moving her chair as far away from him as possible while still being able to see her computer.

"You know you want it girl," Malcolm said in a taunting tone, putting his foot under the chair and pulling it back towards him. His legs were apart. He took hold of both arms of the chair and pulled it towards him, locking her in with his knees.

He grabbed her ponytail as she tried to move but she managed a faint scream before he put his hand over her mouth.

The door burst open and there was a scuffle. Malcolm was on the floor. Someone had his hands behind his back. Their knee in the back of his neck. He had his cheek pressed against the cold floor. He saw Patrick at the door.

"The bloody intercom is on. The whole rig heard what you have been saying, you bloody stupid man. Get your stuff packed and get off my rig today."

Jessica thought she had turned the intercom off.

However, Malcolm had sat on the button when he perched himself on the desk, flicking it from the 'off' position to 'on'.

A Present For The medic

Rig moves were an inevitable part of working offshore.

The North Sea Tiger prefers the static stability of a rig. It is the marine mariners who prefer to bob about on the stormy ocean waves with stomachs of steel which normal people would liken to a day at a theme park.

The rig was moving.

The air of anticipation was rife with a possible move day. Only the offshore 'first-timers' were excited, the others treated it much differently; the nausea, the seasickness, no internet and no phone.

Maryanne's relief refused to do tows, it made him ill, which bemused her as he would boast constantly of his ten years in the Australian Navy before coming offshore.

The day soon came, it was time to sail.

It was not a good start. Maryanne opened the sickbay door to see a burly rig floor worker looking pale and squeamish. He didn't speak but mumbled some pathetic incomprehensible words. He didn't move either but opened his mouth and projected his stomach contents at the medic. The vomit bounced off her chest and onto the surrounding walls.

The worker said nothing. He just stood there with vomit on his beard.

After she had screamed and shouted at him, making sure he felt even worse than he already did, Maryanne sent him to his cabin to rest. The smell made her feel sick.

Just another day in the sickbay.

She hoped the day was over but no such luck as one of the 'third party' girls came to see her. Maryanne was in her pyjamas watching *Coronation Street* when the knock came on her door. It was a gentle knock, not anxious.

"Hi Sandy, what can I do for you?" asked Maryanne.

"Oh, I feel so light-headed," said the rather sad but guilty-looking girl.

"Let's get you into the sickbay," said Maryanne with little enthusiasm. She followed the girl into the room.

She then watched as the girl made a pathetic attempt to faint and fell to the floor. It was so false that Maryanne had to put her hand to her mouth to stop herself laughing.

She waited until the girl had made herself 'comfortable' on the floor before stepping forward and nudging her with her foot.

"Get up you silly girl," said Maryanne.

After several prods, the girl opened one eye.

"Hey, I have fainted you know, I can't possibly get up," she said sadly.

Maryanne sat at her desk, arms crossed.

"Get up off the floor now! That was a very unconvincing attempt at fainting."

The girl jumped to her feet and fixed her hair.

"You're such a bitch Maryanne," she whined, sticking her fingers up at the medic as she stormed out of the room and up the corridor.

"Cured," said Maryanne, laughing as she turned the lights out and locked the door.

Finally.....

Well, where are they today?

There will always be the '*Alecs*'; those who are taken from us in tragic circumstances, reminding everyone how offshore workers 'take a chance' every time they set foot on a helicopter, how short life is, and how precious the time is we have with the ones we love.

The '*Maryanne's*' will never cease to exist. Always on the lookout for the next best thing. Looking to love and be loved, dealing with their demons in their own way – coping, as we all do. They may teeter on the edge but they will always just keep a head above water. Most adults have a bit of 'Maryanne' in them; pretending all is perfect as they struggle to stop their world crumbling around them.

There will always be a '*Todd*' no matter where you work. The academically able; their brains ahead of their feet, trying to fit in. They will stumble and fall, just not quite sure how to 'get there'. They may be told to be academic but they'd be happier in a manual job. Let your kids be who they are; you'll see something beautiful grow.

The big bad '*Brendan's*'. A big ball of wool or yarn will run out eventually. Many would love the best of both worlds but it never lasts; it's a one-way street, a dead end.

'*Nancy*, the survivor'. Little in shell, but strong in mind. This type is forever trying to please their family, never really telling them what they actually want. You could say that a 'Nancy' portrays many offshore workers who just 'fit in' at home.

We probably all know a *'Morgan'* but may not know their 'secret'. The reserved family man next door. Quiet and unassuming but with a rip-roaring secret life that would make for the best revelations at any dinner party.

Maybe one of the saddest characters is *Ugly*. This type of person just pretends to cope, to be the 'North Sea Tiger'. They won't share their inner turmoil, they'll just cope. Their aim is to keep strong without the use of alcohol or drugs. Muddle along, just as they were brought up to do.

How many *'Stevens'* are there out there?

Where do convicted criminals go when released? Do they all reinvent themselves in order to succeed? I expect there are thousands of 'Stevens' out there. Good luck to them.

'Patricks'? I know a few. Married, happy, settled. Well, that's what they portray. Their 'real' sexuality was suppressed through parental pressure at an early age. Eventually, they'll reach an age when they become in tune with their inner selves. They may feel guilty and ashamed, leading to secret meetings with like-minded people, unable to be themselves in society.

'Married, gay' websites are big business. I wonder why.

The media is full of *'Mable'* stories and there will be many 'Mable's' out there. Both male and female. In a life of misery.

I wonder how many *'Sally's'* there are. Would you go that extra mile to help a stranger?

As long as there is offshore work, there will always be a '*Katrina*' and there will always be a '*Jessica*' too. Some are luckier than others but there is always the chance that it will all disappear overnight. Best to love people, not possessions.

The less we say about the '*Arthurs*' in this world the better. We must all remain vigilant. They come in all shapes and sizes.

Oh, and '*Sam the gigolo*'. Waiting in every dark corner of wealthy suburbs and towns, preying on bored and affluent wives. They are easily found online or in newspaper ads. They will never go away as long as the sun sets and the moon rises. We may have evolved as humans but the 'Sams', both males and females, use the easiest and most available 'ticket' for money, just as they have done since Roman times. Good sex in all its shapes and forms has won, and lost many battles. They will always be there, waiting for the 'Katrina's' of this world.

I hope everyone has a '*Joshua*'. They may be a little boy or a little girl, a son or a daughter, or the child of a relative or friend. Even a beloved pet. They might be an adult that cares about you. They are our reason for' taking the chance' to work offshore. To enhance their lives and to make things just a little better in our tough and unfair world.

The wedding was now a memory. It was almost six months since the event.

Terry was in the Arrivals Lounge. He chatted briefly to the leaving OIM.

He had been promoted.

He looked at the crowded lounge and began his 'hello' speech.

"Welcome on board everyone. For those who don't know me, my name is Terry, the OIM."

He nodded to Maryanne who was standing on the other side of the glass partition in the corridor.

"Hey Terry, how did the wedding go? What's your missus called again?" shouted one of the drill floor crew from the back of the room.

Terry looked at the glass again. Maryanne had gone. He looked at his reflection and then at the faces in the room.

"It's Stephanie," he sighed, "her name is Stephanie."

"Well, congratulations to you both," said the lad.

"Back to Narnia," Terry muttered to himself as he made his way to his cabin with his bags.

In my Opinion,

It's not a weakness to keep some things to yourself. Sometimes, just sometimes, it can be for the best.

www.lulu.com / David P Matheson.

Amazon.com.

Google search: David P Matheson Author.

Copyright
Please Don't Go Offshore daddy.

Second Edition.
Copyright 2018.
David P Matheson.
ISBN: 978-0-244-72532-7
Paperback edition 2018.
This work is licensed under the creative commons attribution- share Alike 30.
Un ported License. To view a copy of this license, visit
Or send a letter to:
Creative Commons
171 Second Street, Suite 300
San Francisco, California 94105

USA.